Miranda stood in the candlelit bedroom

Clearly the room was set for seduction. Disbelief—and excitement—coursed through Colin. Was this the same Miranda he'd had snowball fights and pizza parties with when they were kids?

"Shh—no talking..." she said.

She approached him and he felt his groin tighten. The sheer gown she wore hid next to nothing, and he knew he'd have a hard time resisting her.

"Miranda..."

She stepped up close, her breasts grazing his chest as she unbuttoned his shirt. One hand slipped inside the garment and rubbed lightly over his chest. She had to feel the slamming of his heart against his ribs. "Maybe we should slow down...."

She smiled. "Well, we do have all night...."

Her breathing was shallow, and Colin knew she was as aroused as he was. His head was spinning as she peeled off the nightgown. He tried to speak, but the words came out as a groan.

Standing before him in only a silky thong, Miranda met his gaze with such desire, such openness...such passion. Yet he knew with painful clarity that if he let this happen they would regret it later.

He had to end this. *Now.*

Dear Reader,

It's true that the best romantic relationships rest on a solid foundation of friendship, but what about when friendship becomes the biggest obstacle to romance? That's the difficult situation Miranda Carter finds herself in, and her solution to the problem is unique, to say the least.

This book was a lot of fun to write. Writing about friendship and romance gave me opportunity to explore how the two can be a wonderful yet messy combination. Miranda has to figure out how far she is willing to go to get something—or someone—she wants. Who hasn't made an impulsive decision and then had to dig themselves out of the resulting mess? And when the mess means you are having the relationship of your life with the guy you've loved forever, who wants out?

Miranda finds herself in over her head while involved in a fun and sexy romance with Colin, and she learns a lot about herself along the way. I hope you enjoy her journey as much as I did. Stop by my Web site at www.samanthahunter.com and drop me a note letting me know what you think of *About Last Night....*

Sincerely,

Samantha Hunter

Books by Samantha Hunter

HARLEQUIN BLAZE
142—VIRTUALLY PERFECT

ABOUT LAST NIGHT...

Samantha Hunter

TORONTO • NEW YORK • LONDON
AMSTERDAM • PARIS • SYDNEY • HAMBURG
STOCKHOLM • ATHENS • TOKYO • MILAN • MADRID
PRAGUE • WARSAW • BUDAPEST • AUCKLAND

Many thanks to my niece Jessica Bussiere and Julie Cohen
for sharing details about Portland, Maine.

Special thanks to Theresa Stevens for her legal expertise
on sexual harassment and to Dave Susman, Larissa Estell and Cara Summers
for letting me pester them with early drafts.

Most of all, my deepest appreciation to Birgit Davis-Todd, my insightful
and generous editor. Birgit, working with you is a joy, and you really
know how to make a book (and an author) sing! Thank you!

ISBN 0-373-79177-1

ABOUT LAST NIGHT...

1

"So WHEN ARE YOU GOING to jump Colin?"

Her friend Penny's voice was loud, and the women sitting nearby in the beauty salon had ears like bats. Miranda Carter cringed, praying that Penny's voice had been drowned out by the sound of the blow dryers and the salon's Muzak. Otherwise, word would be out all over the small seaside city of Portland, Maine, that she was after Colin Jacobs even before her gold highlights took.

"Shh! Like that's going to happen anytime soon. Or at all."

"You can do anything you set your mind to. I have faith in you."

Before Miranda could reply, Penny had pushed her whole head up under the dryer, so she wouldn't be able to hear Miranda's objections anyway.

Oh, well. It still felt good to be able to spend time with her friend and pamper herself. The highlighting was expensive, but she deserved a treat. It had been a tough year: she'd kicked it off by almost dying, and now she was opening her own business. Not to mention she was living back in Portland again after being gone for almost ten years. Sure, she'd come back for holidays and the occasional birthday, but she hadn't lived here since she'd left for college. It was kind of weird. Nice, but she was still getting used to the idea.

She flexed her leg, stretching it as best she could in the chair. Penny's head popped out again, her usually impish eyes concerned. "Leg hurt?"

Miranda nodded and rubbed it, gesturing to Penny to get back under the dryer. She was fine, the pain was just a residual effect of a compound fracture that was mostly healed but would take much more time to mend completely.

Six months ago she'd been in Denver, where she'd lived since graduating from Colorado State. She'd thought she knew the lower trails by Gray's Peak well enough to risk a weekend hike by herself. A violent autumn thunderstorm had sent her sliding down a slippery slope, proving how wrong she was with a vengeance.

The accident had shaken her badly. The two days of struggling in the cold and rain were thankfully a painful blur. She'd dragged herself over the dirt and rock, searching for her cell phone to call for help, unaware of the extent of her injuries. Apparently she had passed out while trying to call 911, but the signal, though weak, had led an emergency rescue team to her.

When she'd awakened in the hospital her parents had been there, worried to death. When she was out of critical condition, she'd been transported back to Maine, where her folks had helped her to recuperate. At first she'd planned to return to Denver, but she discovered she'd missed Portland more than she'd thought.

Besides, there was nothing really keeping her in Denver. She'd ended a romance that was going nowhere a year before her accident, so there wasn't anyone there waiting for her. But there was someone here in Maine, and that had influenced her decision to stay, though she wasn't ready to admit it, not even to Penny.

Looking out the window at the fading snows of early April, she found it hard to believe her life had changed so much so quickly. She was almost completely healed and happy to be alive, period, but a near-death experience changed the way you looked at things, corny as it sounded. She deeply appreciated simple joys, like getting her hair done with her best friend, in a way she never had prior to the accident.

Her thoughts about things like falling in love felt more urgent. Though she'd always been one to try new things and believed in living life to the fullest, her accident had somehow unleashed a passion for living. That passion was particularly powerful when she thought about Colin Jacobs, and she wanted to do something about it—something that she'd failed to do such a long time ago.

The tumble down the side of the mountain had also shaken more than her romantic sensibilities. She'd been drifting through life, working odd jobs since college, not really knowing what she wanted to do. While in the hospital she'd had a lot of time to think about it, and she knew she wanted to make a difference. The sight of the big brown eyes that were the first thing she'd seen when the rescue team found her—the dogs had reached her first—had inspired her to open her own dog-training school.

It was surprising she hadn't thought of it before. For years she'd been volunteering at animal shelters and with dog trainers, helping to train abandoned pooches to behave better so that they could find homes. She loved working with animals and was good at it. She read about animal behavior, but also followed her instincts, and she'd done pretty well. She'd never thought of combining that experience with her business degree.

Her own two dogs, Chuck and Lucy, were so well trained that people always commented on how nicely behaved they were, and she was proud of that. Not being one to move slowly, once the idea struck her, Miranda had practically cleaned out her bank account to open a small office close by the veterinary office where Penny worked in south Portland. Open for just a little more than two months now, she was receiving referral customers steadily. The accident had nearly killed her, but in many ways it had gotten her to focus on just what her priorities were.

Turning her attention again to the magazine she was holding, she smirked at the cover story—"The Total Seduction: A Five-Step Plan to Jump-Start Your Love Life (or Your Lover)." She didn't even have a lover to seduce—yet—though she had plenty of fantasies rolling around in her lust-saturated brain. She knew that what she needed was a plan to make those fantasies reality. No more waiting around for love to happen.

Colin was an old friend, true, but he also could melt her bones with just a glance. His sparkling golden eyes seduced her constantly and he didn't have a clue. But things between her and Colin were…complicated. At least for her. They'd known each other since kindergarten; they had a lot of history, and that history had a habit of getting in the way of something more developing between them. When she'd come home, it was very much like old times—she and Penny, Colin and Travis, all back together again. She saw Colin all the time; in fact, he'd helped her move her mammoth desk into her office. The four of them usually got together at least once a week. But he didn't really *see* her as a woman, certainly not as a lover—just as his old pal Miranda. It was beyond frustrating.

The hairstylist returned, lifting the hot dryers off their heads. She checked under the foil, blessedly proclaiming them both "done." Miranda grimaced inwardly. She hadn't been *done* in quite a while. Looking down at the magazine, she knew that one way or another she was going to have to change that. And soon.

COLIN BARELY AVOIDED the ball that whipped by his face and smashed into the wall behind him. He nimbly ducked, swung around, sweeping his arm in a powerful arc that sent the small blue ball whizzing across the court and back at Travis, who made an expert corner play back in Colin's direction. Sweat soaked his shirt, and he dragged the back of his fist across his forehead, squinting to focus. Travis was on a brutal tear, and Colin knew he wasn't going to win this one.

Travis, recently returned from medical school in New York, was almost a full-fledged doctor now, and pulling long shifts in rotating departments at the hospital. Colin was amazed that his friend had time or energy for things like racquetball, but Travis never seemed short of energy.

Sometimes their games of handball were low-key, a friendly volley with casual conversation, and other times, like tonight, they were all-out war. Jumping up, Colin fiercely pursued the ball, slamming into the scuffed white wall but missing the shot by a hair.

"Ha! Game! You suck!" Travis had won and, in keeping with tradition, he continued with the humiliating "I won, you lost" song and dance around the court. Colin chuckled, thinking Travis's dance was more embarrassing for himself than it was to Colin— not that Travis was ever embarrassed about anything.

Colin was competitive, too, and he liked to win, but tonight he'd just wanted to push his body to exhaustion to loosen tense muscles. Teaching psychology to undergrads at the university along with doing his own research projects often left him feeling like a spring that had been wound too tight by the end of the day. So he pursued several physical activities to unwind. The body had to be exercised as well as the mind.

He slumped down to the floor and watched Travis

boogie around. Colin looked skyward after hearing giggles floating down from the ceiling. About a dozen female undergrads were watching them from the observation deck. He waved a tired salute, recognizing one of the faces from his freshman psych seminar, and the giggles increased. Great. Travis looked up and then extended a hand to him. Colin grabbed it, pulling himself up.

"They want you, man. They're hot for teacher."

Colin laughed and ducked as Travis chucked the ball at him, hitting the wall to his side.

"Yeah, right. I don't think so."

Travis smacked the ball again, glancing up at the girls. "Chicks that age dig older men, especially their professors. It's all that power and mystery. Haven't you ever been tempted?"

Colin jumped forward, swiping at the ball before Travis could hit it.

"Making time with a student? God, no. For one thing, I could lose my job, and for another, well, you know, it would be like you looking at your patients as prospective dates. I just don't see them that way. They're just students."

Travis grunted as he lunged for the ball.

"I knew some students who dated professors in school. Seems like it goes on a lot, even though they have the so-called rules. Academic policy doesn't really restrain human nature or raging hormones. Depending on the circumstances, I don't see the problem with it, as long as it's mutual."

"Yeah, well, it's not my thing. I prefer women my own age."

"Graduate students, then?"

Colin grabbed the ball out of midair before Travis could pop it back against the wall and pinned his friend with an inquisitive stare. "Why all this sudden curiosity about whether I'm letching after my students?"

Travis looked up again, smiling at the girls, setting off another wave of bubbly laughter. "Just curious. I mean, look at them. They're cute. It's not the same as me with patients. My people are sick, and they are coming to me for help. That's totally different. Even if you don't *do* anything, I can't believe you don't look. I mean, even *think* about it."

Colin rolled his eyes, giving in. "I might notice if they're pretty, sure—"

"Ha! Dawg! I knew it!"

Colin chucked the ball at Travis, bouncing it off his forehead. "But I've *never* thought about a student in a sexual way. I like women who have lived a little, you know, who have more life experience."

"I'm willing to bet some of those girls have had considerable experience."

"Is your mind always in your pants? Or someone else's?"

Travis laughed and shook his head. "Only when I'm off duty."

"And only when you're around Penny?"

Travis's jaw dropped, and he stared at Colin. "Huh?"

"Well, it's obvious you're totally into her. Might as

well come clean." Colin grinned and watched Travis shift uncomfortably. He rarely got Travis on the ropes, and it was fun.

Travis didn't answer right away as they exited the court, and Colin was even more intrigued. When he looked over, his friend's face was as serious as he had ever seen it.

"Okay, yeah. I'm crazy about her. When I got back I asked her out once and it didn't go well. She freaked, so I backed off and we never talk about it."

"Why'd she freak?"

"I don't know. She just got all stressed and I told her not to worry about it. Though now I wish I'd pushed it a little more. I guess it was because of her father leaving them, and her and her mom being on their own, or whatever. I don't know. She can be crazy sometimes, but it's cute."

"You know it's love when crazy is cute. How come you never said anything about asking her out?"

"I only like to brag about my conquests, not my rejections, dude. How about you? Any non-student hotties I should know about?"

They walked through the gym doors and grabbed towels from a fresh stack by the door. Colin sat down on the wooden bench, shaking his head.

"Too busy. I was seeing that woman I told you about in the anthropology department, Sophie, for a while, but she took off to Europe on a grant project, and since then, well, no one's really caught my eye." *Except for Miranda,* the little voice in his head taunted him. He ignored it.

"You know, I always thought you and Miranda would get together."

Colin nearly choked as he heard the words come out of Travis's mouth.

"Excuse me?"

They headed to the showers, and Travis shrugged. "No reason, just that it would be cool if we ended up as couples, you know, me and Pen and you and Randi. We would get married and then our kids would all play together like we did."

Colin turned the shower on full blast, enjoying the wash of heat against his sore shoulders. "Maybe you and Penny could work, but Randi and I could never be more than friends."

Travis tossed him the soap, his brow furrowed inquisitively. "Why not? Are you interested?"

Colin shrugged. "Even if I were, it's out of the question."

Travis shut off the water and grabbed his towel, cinching it around his waist. "Hey, if you want her, man, you should go for it. You guys would be good together. Randi's a doll."

"She is, but it's not in the cards. Besides, I could never know for sure."

"Know what?"

Colin scrubbed the towel over his body, looking away at nothing in particular. "If she was with me or if she was with Derek's brother."

"What the heck does that mean?"

"Think about it. She was in love with Derek. You

know that. She was devastated when he died. We all were. I figured that's why she left and never came back much. Even if it were a remote possibility for us to get together, I would always be second string, Trav. That's not good enough."

"I don't know, Col. I may be off base, but it seemed that when we got together the other night there was definite chemistry working between you two. We were all dancing, but you two kept gravitating back to each other. High school is a world away—you've barely seen each other for years—you're like brand-new people now."

"You can't just erase the past, Trav. I mentioned something about Derek to her, and I could see it in her face. Something changed in her eyes. I don't think she ever quite got over him. If we danced a lot together the other night it was just because you kept trying to maneuver Penny into that dark corner."

"Yeah, not very successfully. I do like watching her dance, though."

Colin smiled at Travis and turned back toward the lockers. In spite of the vigorous exercise, talking about Miranda had stirred up the feelings he was trying to exorcise. As his skin heated with familiar waves of desire, he wondered if being second best would be better than nothing at all, or if it would be worse.

MIRANDA AND PENNY SAT crunched into a small booth at their favorite waterfront pub. The place had been around when their parents had been kids and was still going strong. The heady aroma of garlic and freshly baked pizza permeated the air and had made Miranda's mouth water as always when she'd walked through the door. Though she'd sat in this booth a hundred times, everything seemed sweeter, more pungent now.

She looked around, soaking up the atmosphere. They had been working on a large pizza for the past hour, and finally the subject that had been left behind at the salon reemerged.

"So, what's your plan for dealing with the Colin situation?"

"I don't know. I haven't really thought about it."

Penny sent her a definite "oh, c'mon" look across the table, and she caved.

"Okay, I have been thinking about it, but thinking and doing are two different things."

"The other night you two seemed to have some real sizzle going. He asked you to dance."

Miranda shrugged. "Yeah, but the four of us danced together. I danced with Travis as much as Colin, so did you. Colin and I are close, and he's been great since I've been back." She sighed, shaking her head. "Every now and then I do think I catch a little sense of something more, something different between us, but I think it's just me and wishful thinking."

Miranda looked intently at the pizza and seriously considered another slice. Nerves made her want to eat and she had plenty of them. Thank God for elliptical trainers and a fast metabolism.

Grabbing the slice, she took a bite to avoid continuing and then reached down into her bag, taking out the magazine from the salon. She met Penny's questioning eyes squarely. "What? They said I could take it."

"Did you tell them you wanted it for a recipe?" Penny's eyes danced with evil mirth as she glanced over the cover story. "Or is this research?"

"It was an interesting article." Miranda slumped back in her seat, pizza forgotten. "Yeah, okay. It got me thinking about Colin. What doesn't? I want to do something, but I don't want to lose him as a friend. It's driving me crazy. I would have thought I was over this a long time ago. Then *wham,* since I've been back it's been full-force adult lust. Very frustrating."

Penny squeezed her hand and smiled before she resumed eating her pizza. "You're such a romantic. It doesn't surprise me that you feel this way. You were crazy about him then. Going out with Derek was a mistake."

"I know. I guess I just thought since one brother wasn't interested, maybe the other one would do. Or in truth, I was hoping to make Col jealous, though I know it was awful to use Derek that way. And I know he used to rub Col's face in it, but I thought maybe that would jar him, make him come around, but I guess he really didn't have those feelings for me. Then or now. But I look at Colin still and it's like…"

"Everything else disappears?" Penny finished her sentence, and shared her own insights.

"Colin always had that extra, I don't know what to call it. He was just…deeper. I mean, he's gorgeous, but he's also a nice guy. Rare combination."

"I know. He's almost *too* nice, though." Miranda grimaced. "I wish I could get him to be a little naughty."

"I think he was always trying to make up for Derek. Derek was great, but he was such a bad boy. God, remember how he gave Joyce and Ed fits?" Penny laughed softly, remembering the good old days. "He was always in trouble. And he was just as gorgeous as Colin, but I can see how Colin would have felt like he had to behave, you know, to balance out Derek."

Penny sighed, tipping her empty bottle at the server to indicate she would like another before continuing. "You know, after you left, it was so sad. He got sucked up in school and taking care of his parents. He and I hung out a little, but we didn't have much in common."

"Why not? You've known him as long as any of us, and you were in school, too."

Penny's mouth twisted self-derisively. "Hardly the same as what you guys were doing."

"Penny, you got a good two-year degree, you graduated at the top of your class, and you're doing a job you love, not to mention you're great at it. You're amazing with those animals. And with the people, too. Don't sell yourself short."

"Yeah, being a vet's assistant is fun, but it's hardly like being a doctor or a professor. Or having your own business. Speaking of which, how's that going?"

"Good so far. Starting up is slow, but I owe my ability to pay the rent to you. With the clients you're sending my way, I'm getting more referrals and business is picking up. It was a good idea to set up shop so close by the vet's. A lot of folks seem to walk their dogs in that area, too." She lifted her beverage in a salute to Penny, and continued. "I think I may start some group classes at the shelter, and split the proceeds with them. I need to do more formal training in some advanced techniques, though, so I can maybe pick up some contract work with the police, or search-and-rescue teams. Then maybe I can afford to do some free classes for people who can't afford to pay."

"That's good thinking. I'm glad it's going well for you—you deserve it. If you could get things going with Colin, life would be almost perfect, huh?"

Miranda considered what Penny had told her about Colin. "I hate it that he sees me as Derek's girlfriend instead of just me."

Penny nodded. "Then I guess you have to tell him. I can see why you wouldn't have said anything right away, but I think it's time to tell him you'd actually broken up with Derek the night of the accident and see if it makes a difference. It could clear the air for something to happen between you two."

"Ha! Talking to him directly? I don't know about that plan—far too much fall-flat-on-my-face potential. That would be too sensible and straightforward for me." She smiled reluctantly over her drink. "Why do you always make sense?"

"Hey, that's me. Sensible Penny. Just like the loafers."

"Stop it. You are as wildly lacking in sense as the rest of us, and I won't hear any differently. Hey, a couple guys at the bar haven't been able to take their eyes off you all night. You are such a sex goddess."

Penny grinned and looked toward the bar, her green eyes impish. She *was* cute—the type of woman men were automatically attracted to. A small, pixielike redhead, Penny had an innate, feminine sex appeal that Miranda sometimes envied. Miranda liked her own straight, statuesque build well enough—being strong and streamlined had its own advantages—but sometimes she wished she was curvier and cuter like her friend.

A laugh bubbled up from Penny when she waved playfully at the guys at the bar. Penny routinely underestimated herself, which Miranda found frustrating. She knew it came from the fact that Penny had grown up in less comfortable circumstances than the rest of them, but it bugged her that Penny insisted on downplaying herself much of the time.

"Yeah, I'm a real sex kitten."

"Hmm. Maybe one who's interested in curling up in the lap of one particularly cute resident doctor that we both happen to know."

"*Eww!* Hardly. Though maybe I'd like to scratch him."

"Why do you even bother to hide it? You guys are obviously hot for each other."

"Um, Miranda, have you been in a room with us lately—or, come to think of it—ever?"

"Actually, yes. You argue like cats and dogs, but that is just the adult version of the playground-punch-in-the-arm. Face it, you're a smitten sex kitten."

"Puh-leese. Clever way to sidetrack this conversation, but let's get back to you."

"Coward. I still say if you made a move on Travis, he'd cave like a house of cards. I, on the other hand, am facing the sexual Berlin Wall with Colin."

"Well, you know, they did tear that down, so there's hope."

"Okay, fine, Great Wall of China then, smart aleck." She grimaced playfully. "I have to think of something. If I store up any more sexual energy I am going to explode. And it won't be pretty."

"So are you seriously thinking of implementing the five-step plan here?" Penny gestured at the cover story in the magazine lying between them.

Miranda took another bite of her pizza and chewed, mulling that idea. "Maybe. Some of the ideas were good. And if it doesn't work, I can at least say I tried. Life's too short to be wishy-washy about things. You just gotta jump in and see what happens."

She didn't really feel that casual about it—the feelings she had for Colin were strong, if confusing, and if he rejected her, it would hurt. But she'd survive. She'd discovered that about herself: she was a survivor.

There was something about quiet, responsible Colin that made her want to burrow down under the layers and see what was there. She wanted to release the wild man underneath all that calm. If she could do it, she had a feeling it would be worth the risk.

She couldn't believe it when she'd returned home

and he was still here and single. But he was different. Grown-up, a man now, and even more gorgeous than she'd remembered. Those tawny, hazel eyes seemed to stare straight through her, and though she knew it was corny, she longed for the kind of deep connection that she imagined a woman could have with a man like that. The kind that lasted forever.

Penny reached over and waved the magazine in front of Miranda's face. "Earth to Miranda, so what's step one?"

"They suggest a woman should take control of the relationship as a first move. No waiting around for the guy to decide, or to make up his mind about when and where. You decide how, you decide where, you decide when. Men have always been under pressure to make these big decisions, and they face rejection all the time. So, you relieve pressure by being the one to take control. It's supposed to energize your relationship and push things to a new level."

Putting the magazine back down on the table, Penny nodded approvingly.

"Sounds good. How do you do that, exactly?"

"They have several suggestions, from simply inviting him out on a date to doing a striptease, or setting up a seduction, including bondage and other kinky stuff that is control related. It depends on the existing relationship you have with the other person, and your personalities. Something tells me Colin would run for the hills if I pulled out the handcuffs."

Penny's eyes widened. "You have handcuffs?"

"I was speaking hypothetically, Pen."

"Oh. Well, sounds like it's worth a try."

Miranda felt a naughty smile twitch at the corners of her lips. Her mind was made up. Her skin tingled with excitement. She had her plan in hand. She was going to seduce Colin Jacobs.

2

Colin,
Come to my house at seven tonight—I have a surprise for you. Come alone, and you can't say a word until I tell you to. Oh, and don't be late. I know this probably sounds strange, but just do it. Remember, no talking!
Randi

COLIN STARED at Miranda's e-mail in the dim light of his office. Books were stacked everywhere and piles of student tests cluttered his desk, leaving just enough room for the laptop that glowed in the darkness. To the outside observer it looked like a complete mess, but he knew exactly what was in every spot. Research projects, student papers, faculty documents—he could find anything he needed quickly. Why bother with extras like filing cabinets? But at the moment, he simply narrowed his eyes as he read the screen, murmuring to himself.

"No talking? Just do it? What the heck is she up to?"

His curiosity was piqued. It had been two nights

since he'd seen Travis and discussed his feelings for Miranda. Maybe Travis was right—maybe he should just take a chance. God knows he'd thought about it enough. But as soon as he seriously considered it, the same heaviness would settle in his gut and he couldn't go through with it. Quick affairs were nice, and he'd had his share of them, but with Miranda it would have to be something more. He knew they could never really have a future together. And worse, their friendship could be destroyed in the process.

He could hear his brother Derek's voice in his head as clear as if it were yesterday, bragging about how he and Miranda were dating, and how they had made out for hours in the back seat of his car. It had driven Colin nuts, but his brother had beaten him to her and there was nothing to be done about it. The best man—or at least the braver man—had won.

Colin hadn't been completely honest with Travis. He'd thought about approaching Randi a million times since she'd returned home, had played out what he would say, how he might ask her out, and it had never felt right. In his head, she was his brother's girl, not his. She was only Colin's in his fantasies, which had been long dead until she returned, when they had refueled with an almost cruel ferocity.

He closed his eyes and pictured her, feeling his insides tighten and his skin go warm. She was almost his height—nearly six feet—slim, and strong. She had...presence. There was intelligence in her face and, God knows, her voice alone could inspire his fantasies for nights on end.

She was beautiful, no doubt, with long, curling sable hair that tumbled everywhere and deep brown eyes that didn't miss a thing. He'd often dreamed about wrapping those tresses around his hands, or burying his face in them. But she was more than beautiful.

She had a kind of fire that always seemed to be burning just under the surface, a quiet intensity. Yet she was one of the most open and friendly people he knew. If only he could bring himself to take the chance—

"Dr. Jacobs?"

Shaken out of his reverie, he looked up and saw Nell, his teaching assistant, standing in the doorway. It was getting dark outside and he switched the small desk lamp on, glancing at his watch. He was due at Miranda's soon. He was curious as to what had prompted her to send that strange e-mail telling him to show up but remain silent. Probably Penny and Travis were in on whatever it was as well.

"Hello, Nell. What can I do for you?"

She stepped tentatively into the office, laying a stack of papers down on the desk.

"These are done. I applied the grading criteria you gave me as best I could, but I marked some of the ones that were less clear with Post-its for your review."

He smiled. Nell was a first-year doctoral student in clinical psychology, and she worked hard—maybe too hard. Her straight black hair was pulled back tightly from her face and she wore no makeup, not even lipstick. Shadows showed under her eyes. It made her appear very...sparse. And exhausted.

"I appreciate you getting these to me so quickly, but you could have taken a little longer. I know you just got out of your own version of midterm hell. How are your classes going?"

She bit her lip, looking down.

"Oh, they're fine. Quantitative stats is giving me a little bit of a problem, but I'll get through it."

"You will. Smythe is tough, but she's a great professor. I'd be happy to help you with some of the problem sets if you get stuck, just let me know. Quantitative is important."

She nodded and turned her head to glance out the window that overlooked the quad.

"You're here pretty late. I didn't expect you to be in, but figured I would leave the tests on your desk for morning."

"Yes, well, I'm trying to get through this grading. There may be a few students from your section I'll need to confer with you about before this is over."

She smiled, and he thought she might actually be pretty if she tried.

"Okay, just let me know when you need me to do that. I am usually near e-mail."

He was eager to draw their conversation to a close, but wanted to be supportive. "You're doing a great job, Nell. Above and beyond. Tell you what, let me take you for a coffee next week and we'll talk about the tests in a more pleasant place than the office. Sound good?"

She nodded awkwardly and in the low light he could just see pink stain her cheeks as she backed away from the desk. He stepped around the desk, looking at his watch again, and knew he had to hurry her out of the office if he was going to make it to Miranda's in time.

"Listen, I remember what it was like, and I want us to have a different kind of relationship than I had with my advisor. Hopefully a much more friendly one."

He slipped a companionable arm around her shoulders and guided her to the doorway, needing to hasten her departure so he could leave. He gave her arm a quick squeeze before reaching for his jacket. Her eyes widened and she nodded before saying a quick good-bye and exiting the room. He shook his head, hoping he'd gotten his point across. This was the first semester he had had his own teaching assistant, and he didn't want to get a reputation as an ogre.

He was all for hard work, but sometimes if you overdid it, your production could actually suffer. He saw it happen all the time in burned-out students and colleagues. Other advisors had their T.A.s over to dinner, and created more of a social situation, treating them like colleagues more than students. He made a mental note to make more of an effort in that area. Coffee would be a start.

He shut down the laptop. It was later than he had thought, and he had to get going. Closing up his briefcase, he grabbed his jacket and shut the light off behind him, wondering again what Miranda's mysterious e-mail was all about. He expected to find out soon.

MIRANDA HEARD the truck pull up in front of the house and looked out into the lighted driveway, confirming that it was Colin. She peered through the curtain, watching all six feet of him slide out of the heavy-duty pickup, and sucked in a breath. He stood for a moment, as if he wasn't sure what to do, or why he was there, and then closed the truck door.

He wore the years well, the man fulfilling the promise in the boy, his lanky frame filled out, muscular and hard. She watched him approach the door, the muscles of his thighs stretching against his jeans with each long step. Miranda had frequently treated herself to the view of those jeans from behind and quivered in anticipation of seeing what was underneath them. He still fried her brain cells like no other man ever had.

Even though she watched him approach, the knock on the door had Miranda nearly jumping out of her skin. In the twenty minutes or so she'd fussed and waited for Colin to arrive, she'd gone over every move, every detail, many times. He was on time, seven sharp, as she knew he would be. The moment was at hand. She pulled herself up, reminding herself that this was Colin, the man she'd known her entire life, and whom she'd always been attracted to. This could only be good, right?

Forcing herself to relax, she went to her bedroom door, calling to him to come in. She watched him enter the room and look up the stairs, following her voice. When his eyes widened in surprise, traveling down the length of her scantily clad body and back to her face, his mouth opened to speak, but she quickly put a finger to her lips, silencing him.

"No. No talking. Just come up."

It was clear from his expression that whatever he'd been expecting, *this* was not it. She gestured to him to join her with a naughty little tilt of her head, smiling in delicious anticipation. This was going to be fun.

COLIN HEARD the door click shut behind him and swallowed hard as the scent of her sexy perfume wafted over him. He walked up the stairs on automatic pilot, curiosity consuming him. What was going on?

It was clear enough when he saw her, posed sexily in the doorway of her bedroom. He tried to train his eyes in another direction, but the room was clearly set for seduction. Then his gaze landed on her again, disbelief coursing through him. It was almost hard to believe this was Miranda—his Miranda—with whom he'd had snowball wars and late-night pizza parties when they were kids.

She walked up to him and he felt his groin tighten in a way that suggested he was going to have a very hard time resisting her. It was every fantasy he'd ever had about her coming true. The sheer gown she wore hid next to nothing, and it occurred to him that this was the first time he'd seen her naked, or as close to it as he could imagine. Well, there had been that one time they'd all gone skinny-dipping when they were thirteen, but that was not the same at all.

The lacy material clung to her breasts, and was slit nearly to the hip. A long, silken leg emerged as she walked toward him, and he wasn't sure, but he might have groaned out loud.

"Mir—"

"Shh! No talking. I told you."

Her voice was sultry and commanding, and she had a fire in her eyes that sent arrows of lust shooting straight to his…toes. Who would have known he liked having a woman taking control this way, leaving him mute and helpless? With other lovers, he had always been in control, the one who made the moves. He had initiated the action. This was…mildly kinky? To enjoy having someone else be in control, ordering him around? He didn't know he would like kinky sex. But as he felt himself thicken, becoming painfully hard, he knew he liked it quite a lot. He filed that thought away for further examination later.

She stepped up close, her breasts grazing his chest as she pushed the lightweight jacket from his shoulders, then loosened the knot of his tie, which did nothing to clear the obstruction in his throat. She took him by the hand, leading him to a small table. She looked into his eyes, hers communicating brazen desire.

"I'm going to feed you."

He noticed she didn't ask, for instance, *Are you hungry? Would you like a strawberry?* But a statement. A command. He knew he should stand up, call this off, but his mind and his body were too caught up in her spell to object. And who was he kidding? She was every man's fantasy—his in particular—come to life.

She poured a glass of champagne and took a sip,

then dipped a ripe strawberry in the glass before lifting it to his mouth. He took a bite. A drizzle of juice escaped down his chin, and he might have touched an electric fence for the jolt that shot through him as their tongues touched when they both attempted to catch the stray drop. He heard her chuckle, a low, sexy laugh that told him he was in big trouble.

The feeding went on for torturous minutes on end. She not only fed him but let him watch her eat, and he felt his muscles clench in primal response when she dipped her fingers into the champagne and traced them down her chest, along the edges of the nightgown over the creamy curves of her breast. He licked his lips instinctively and felt his traitorous cock throb with need. There was nothing he could do to stop it. She was shredding his control into confetti.

Victory and lust surged in her eyes as she took in his reaction, and she clasped his hand in hers again, pulling him over to the full-length mirror on the other side of the room. He watched them both as she stood beside him, running her hands over him, tugging his shirt loose, buttons popping and flying everywhere.

His heart thundered in his chest. His eyes were glued to the image of her undressing him. He felt as if he was in an excruciatingly seductive dream, except that every tingle of response, every shudder of pleasure as her hands moved over him was achingly real.

She slipped her hands inside his shirt and rubbed them lightly over his chest. She had to feel the slamming of his heart against his ribs. Heat washed over him. It had been far too long for him, and he'd exercised great restraint. Now he was too close to the edge from her simple touch.

Her mouth followed her hands and before he knew it he was naked in front of the mirror, his body glistening with sweat, every inch of him from head to toe rock-hard and fully aroused. He stared at the image of her kneeling in front of him, such a submissive position for a woman so in command.

When her reflection showed her leaning forward to touch her mouth to his already incredibly sensitized erection, he nearly lost it right there. His mind clicked a mental photograph of the picture they made, an image he would never forget. Things were getting out of control—he was out of control—and he needed to stop this. With a grunt of objection, he backed up, away from her mouth. She rose and smiled, taking him by the hand again and leading him to the bed.

"You're right—no need to rush things. We have all night. Sit." Her breathing was shallow, and he knew she was as aroused as he was. It was wrong that he let it go this far, but he was so hungry for her, and he really didn't want to stop, even though that way was madness. He felt his head spin as she peeled off the nightgown. He tried to speak, but the words came out as a long groan.

Standing before him in only a silky, flesh-toned thong, she met his gaze with such desire, such openness, and such...passion...he knew with painful clarity that if he let this happen they would regret it later.

As much as he wanted her, *needed* her, he had to end this.

It was almost physically painful to push down the wanting, to ruthlessly shut off the desire, but he forced himself to do so. She walked to him, concern evident in her expression, lifting her hand to touch him, and he nearly flew to the other side of the room, not trusting himself to be touched one more time and still stay strong.

MIRANDA WATCHED HIM withdraw from her and felt confusion and rejection splash over her like ice water. She stood there, naked, wondering what had gone wrong. Her plan was working. He'd enjoyed it, that was obvious. She knew he wanted her as much as she wanted him. Yet in one second, in one horrible moment, the wall had slammed down between them yet again and he had pulled away, physically and emotionally. Dazed, she couldn't fathom what was happening.

"Colin, I don't understand…" Her voice was barely a whisper and she took a step forward, stopping as he took a step back.

"Miranda…Randi, please. Just give me a minute."

Chills traveled over her skin, followed by a surge of shame and deep embarrassment. She too reached for anything she could to cover up, tears stinging at the back of her eyelids.

"Why? What's wrong?" She wrapped a sheet around her body and tried to manage the tumult of emotions that raged through her. She was shaking and her breath came in gulps, but she fought hard for some vestige of control. She watched him finish dressing and managed to speak again, her voice small, which she hated though she couldn't seem to control it.

"Don't you think I'm sexy, Colin? Don't you want me?"

His head snapped up. She saw the shock in his face, and knew that wasn't it, as he was quick to confirm.

"Does it look like I don't want you? I'm burning with it, Randi, but it just doesn't feel right. I shouldn't have let this happen."

She felt her knees shake beneath her but somehow continued to stand. Staring him in the eye, she demanded an answer.

"Why not? You won't even give it a chance."

Silence hung between them for a long moment, and his jaw squared, as if he were hanging hard on to his control.

"I'm having a physical reaction to you—what man wouldn't? You're gorgeous and seductive, but that's all it is. Just a physical response. And one we shouldn't act on."

"That's all you feel for me? You are just reacting like any man would to a naked woman?" Disbelief and hurt were evident in her words, and he tried to explain.

"I didn't mean it like that. You are my friend and I care about you, and that's why I'm stopping. Try to think about this rationally, Miranda."

Her heart constricted and she wasn't sure she could breathe. *"Rationally?"* She didn't know if she actually spoke the question. She saw red. He was stomping on her heart, humiliating her, rejecting her without even a good reason why.

Colin stepped forward, but this time she retreated.

"Listen, Randi, you may think you want to start something with me, and I can almost understand that. You might see me as an alternate to Derek, a way to put those demons to rest, but that's not a role I intend to take up."

She angrily clutched the sheet more tightly around herself. "You honestly think I wanted to sleep with you as a substitute for Derek? I never even slept with Derek, you moron! How could you think such a thing? Did you get this out of one of your psychology books, Col? If you don't want me, be honest about it, but cut the psychobabble."

"Miranda—"

"We've always had something between us, Colin, whether you will admit it or not. Stay, and give us a chance, Colin, or just get out. It's your choice." Her voice caught, but she stood strong, her eyes blazing into his. He stood helplessly for a moment and then turned away. She closed her eyes, not wanting him to see her heartbreak, but she knew she didn't need to worry about that as she heard the door open and then click softly shut.

"Fine, then. Just go." She spoke to the empty room. Giving in to the pain, she let the sobs take her over.

COLIN PARKED his truck at the side of the road in Old Port, regret gnawing at his gut. If he'd known what she had on her mind he never would have shown up tonight. He'd hurt her, he knew, but she needed to hear the truth before they got caught up in something that wasn't healthy for either of them. He should feel as if he'd done the right thing—so why didn't he?

The streets were quiet, though some folks enjoyed a walk along the old cobblestone streets in the warming spring air. He stopped by a sidewalk bridge between two buildings that overlooked Casco Bay and stared out into the darkness. When Derek had died, he'd gone through the predictable stages of grief—anger at his brother for leaving him alone. And guilt. The horrible frustration and guilt he felt while he watched his parents suffer. No matter what he did, he couldn't make it better.

He couldn't make it better for Miranda, either, then or now. She'd left Portland after Derek's death, and maybe some of those old ghosts were things she still had to work through now that she was home again, but he wasn't going to be part of that. He had to be the one who stayed in control. When she thought things through, she would be glad he had walked away. Even though it was the last thing he'd wanted to do. It would have been so easy to give in, to sink into the willing flesh of her body, have all his fantasies become reality. But what was easy wasn't always right.

"Dammit, Miranda."

He pushed back from the rail and began walking to the car, his mind numb and his body still on fire. He needed a cold shower and some sleep. Maybe he'd wait a few days and then try to talk to her. He only made it a few steps when he heard a funny little squeaking sound and someone yelling. Suddenly, he saw two men on bikes barreling down on him, waving their hands frantically for Colin to get out of the way. They hit their brakes, and he watched their bikes wobble, but it was too late.

He moved to avoid them, but one biker unfortunately moved in the same direction he did. The impact was hard and sudden; he felt the sharp jab of the bike's handles into his gut and then the heavy thud of a body as the man flew over the handles of the bike, crashing into him. Colin was pushed backward, flipping over the rail. Strangely, through the surge of pain and movement, he thought how odd it felt to be so completely out of control of his body for the second time that evening, tossed about as if he were weightless.

He grabbed desperately for the rail but only grasped darkness. The next sensation he felt was intense, bone-biting cold—and pain. He hit something hard, and it hurt. He saw Miranda's face in his mind's eye just as everything faded to black.

3

"I WANT TO SPEAK to Dr. Monroe, Travis Monroe. I want to see him *now!*" Miranda was nearly hysterical with fear, and was willing to walk directly over the emergency nurse and into the intensive care unit if she had to.

They had Colin. Travis had called her, and she had somehow made it to the hospital through her panic and tears. She had to see him, see that he was alive, before she would listen to anyone. She had to see for herself. God, it was all happening again. First with Derek, and now Colin. If they lost him how could she live with herself? Obviously he had been upset when he left. This was all her fault.

The nurse put gentle but firm hands on her shoulders, and Miranda braced herself to break way when she was distracted by footsteps running up behind her. Just at that moment, Travis turned a corner out into the hallway, his expression grave. She started to call to him but saw Colin's mother dash past her, and over to Travis. Miranda broke away and quickly followed behind Colin's dad and Penny.

The scene was sheer chaos. Travis put his hands up to stop the flow of questions that suddenly flooded the hall and herded them back toward the waiting room. Miranda looked at Joyce, Colin's mom, and felt ashamed of her own lack of control. Joyce must be reliving the nightmare of losing Derek right now and that was much worse than her own panic. The older woman was drawn and pale and clearly needed to sit down. Miranda swallowed her fear and dropped back, trailing the group as they entered a small room.

Travis started to speak.

"First things first—you should all relax. Colin's okay. We're watching him carefully right now. He was mildly hypothermic and took a nasty bump, but his vitals are good and he didn't sustain any serious internal injuries or broken bones, which is amazing in and of itself."

Miranda felt relief well in her heart and tears filled her eyes. She glanced over in surprise when she felt a strong hand squeeze hers, and realized Colin's dad, Ed, was holding her hand, his own face tense with worry. She nodded reassuringly at him, squeezing his hand back as Travis continued speaking.

"There is one thing, though. You need to know before you see him."

"What? What is it?" Miranda spoke for the first time, and Travis's eyes locked on hers.

"Well, this isn't unusual with a serious fall, and it will likely clear itself up quickly, but—"

"Just spit it out, Travis!" Penny interrupted impatiently, and Travis slid her a look that made Miranda wince.

"He isn't remembering everything at the moment. He knows he was in the water, but he doesn't remember how he got there, how he was rescued, or the events leading up to the fall." He surveyed their faces, gauging their reactions before he continued. "There could be other random memory loss, but we have to wait and see. Sometimes people will permanently lose their recollections of the events immediately prior to a traumatic experience and other times it comes back in stages. It's confusing for him right now, so just go with it."

Joyce's voice quavered. "Will he know us?"

Travis squeezed her shoulder kindly. "I'm pretty sure he will. At least from what we could tell, it seems he's lost a chunk of time, but not his memories of people. Especially those he's closest to. Besides, who could forget your cooking?"

Miranda admired Travis's professionalism, as well as his kindness. She had never seen him in his doctor role before and was very impressed. He was like an entirely different person. It was hard to believe this was the same carrot-topped, practical-joke-loving Travis they had all grown up with.

"We have to wait until he is fully awake and aware until we know the extent of his memory loss. And he may have some short-term memory problems in the coming days or weeks. That's not unusual with amnesia, so don't worry if he can't remember a phone number, or something like that."

They nodded. Ed guided Joyce over to a couch to sit down, leaving Travis, Penny and Miranda together.

Penny spoke, her wry voice cutting through the tension. "Travis, are you sure? Remember you told me my toe needed to be cut off when I stubbed it?" She reached over and flipped the end of Travis's tie.

Travis's expression was pained as he closed his eyes and shook his head. Leave it to Penny.

"I was twelve then, Pen."

"Yeah, but still, you were *way* wrong."

Miranda had to smile and wink at Penny. A little humor never hurt.

"When can we see him, Travis?"

"You can all go in to see him, one at a time, to put your minds at rest…but just for a minute. He needs to sleep this off. He's pretty heavily sedated, too, so don't expect much. Tomorrow he will be better."

They nodded and proceeded to walk single file down the hallway behind Travis. Miranda caught up with Travis, relieved she could finally speak to him alone.

"You said he was in a bicycle accident. Was anyone else hurt?"

Travis stood by the emergency-room door, stepping to the side while Joyce went in to see Colin.

"The other guy was pretty banged up, has a decent concussion, but his friend managed to avoid the whole thing, which was a blessing. He had an emergency flare and a flashlight on his bike and managed to signal a nearby boat coming in for the night. If Colin had been in the water much longer, his chances would not have been good at all. Hypothermia sets in fast."

Miranda sank against the wall, swallowing hard.

"I can't even imagine how bad this must be for Ed and Joyce. They were supposed to leave on an anniversary cruise in two days. They are probably wrecks."

Travis rubbed his chin thoughtfully. "I'll talk to them when they come out. I can understand their panic, but it's probably not necessary to cancel their trip. Col will feel banged up for a few days, and we'll have to wait and see on the memory issues, but he'll be up and around by tomorrow, and we'll probably release him if he shows no other symptoms."

Miranda considered telling Travis about their evening, wondering if it might help to trigger Colin's memory, then she shut up. Everyone was going to think she was a bad-luck charm for the Jacobs brothers.

Joyce and Ed came back into the hallway appearing much more relaxed, and Travis smiled.

"He was awake? He knew you?"

"Oh, yes. Right away. Though he couldn't say much. When will you be releasing him? He can come home and we'll take care of him."

"You know, Randi here tells me you two had a trip planned. As long as nothing else happens tonight or tomorrow—which it likely won't—" he added at the sight of Joyce's suddenly worried expression "—he'll be fine to get up and go home after a day of observation. The best thing for him to do, and for his memory, is to get back to his normal life as soon as he feels up

to it. With no major injuries, he'll probably want to return to work and a normal routine."

Joyce was doubtful. "Oh, I don't know. I think he
should…"

"Hey, now, you may be the best cookie-baker this
side of the planet, but I'm the doctor, right? Just go
home now, and relax. He's fine. He's lucky."

Ed nodded and shook Travis's hand before leaving.
Miranda watched them, then turned to Travis.

"Do you mind if I go in for a moment? Alone?" She
slid an apologetic look at Penny, who, with her hands,
motioned her to go along.

"You go on in. I'm fine. I'll see him tomorrow when
I can talk with him more. There's no point in tiring him
out now."

Miranda nodded and, with her heart in her throat,
walked into the room, unsure of what she would face
there.

The hall, which had been crowded and noisy, was
suddenly extremely quiet. Penny peeked up at Travis
as she kicked at the corner of the wall.

"So he really is okay? You weren't just trying to
make them all feel better?"

"Penny, doctors really aren't allowed to be less than
completely honest. Unfortunately, even when the news
is bad, we have to tell it like it is. So yes, unless something wildly unusual happens, he really is going to be
fine. We're keeping a close eye on him so don't worry."

She smiled, relieved, and suddenly felt awkward

standing so close to Trav. He'd always been skinny and gawky, freckled and redheaded. She'd called him "Opie" and "chicken legs" and a bunch of other names for as long as she could remember. The teasing was an equalizer between them. It helped erase the fact that Travis's life had been so different from her own.

Travis had been the last of their little group to appear, his parents moving to Portland from New York City when he was seven. His father was a well-known attorney and, though the group lived within blocks of each other, Travis's home was much more luxurious than the rest of theirs. He'd traveled all over the world, spoke two other languages and could discuss topics she had no idea about.

Getting stuck in public school for a year because his parents had missed registration when they moved, Travis was out of his element, away from the posh private schools he had attended in New York. He'd been small, skinny and smart—a prime target for bullying—until Penny, Colin and Miranda had rallied around and taken him into the fold. Travis had completed the group. Colin was the intellectual, Miranda was the adventurer, Penny was the no-nonsense one, and Travis was the clown.

She still recalled how when his parents had tried to register him for private school, he'd pitched a fit to stay where he was, and they'd let him. The Monroes were great. Penny had to admit they had never made her feel out of place or like they were rich and she was poor, though that was the truth of it.

When the four of them played, had parties, or otherwise got together, it was always at one of the others' homes or some other location. The small apartment her mother had just didn't have room for visitors, and besides Penny hadn't really wanted anyone to come over anyhow. She'd slept on the sofa bed in the living room, and her mom in the too-small bedroom. There had been barely room for a desk and a secondhand computer for Penny out in the living room. Miranda had been the only one who ever had visited.

Penny had never wanted Travis to see where she had grown up, though now her mom lived in a modest but pretty home that Penny had helped her buy. It was the least she could do for all the sacrifices her mother had made for her.

She nudged her toe against the wall again and looked at Travis from beneath her long lashes. He was still skinny, but now it was in that lithe I-want-to-start-at-your-ankles-and-crawl-my-way-up-to-your-lips kind of way. His hair fell adorably over his forehead and he was always batting it away from his friendly blue eyes. She loved the color of his hair. Penny was also a redhead, but hers was more strawberry blond, where his was a deep copper. She tried not to notice—honestly she put forth her best effort—but he was just so *hot*.

She also had to put forth her best effort to hide her feelings when other women noticed him—every time they were out in a public place. Travis hadn't been a monk, she knew, but most of his relationships hadn't been under her nose, occurring when he was away at school. He always said residents didn't have time for romance, which must be true, because she hadn't seen him with anyone in a while.

She came back into the moment, grinding her teeth when she saw him grinning at her in that "Ha! You think I'm gorgeous" way that burned her butt. She put her hands on her hips, and faced him squarely.

"What?"

"You know you want me. Why don't you just give in to your desires. Pen? Treat yourself. You deserve it."

She barked out a laugh and rolled her eyes.

"Hey, maybe you can get one of your doctor friends to check out your ego, it seems to be a little swollen."

He simply smiled wider and took a step closer. God, the one thing that hadn't changed was what an annoying smart-ass he could be.

"That's not exactly where I'm feeling some swelling at the moment." His eyes were wicked, and she had to fight a smile.

"You're disgusting."

"C'mon, Penster. Go out with me. How many times are you going to shoot me down?"

Nervously jamming her hands into her pockets, she scowled. "Give it up. I'm never going out with you, Travis. You're not my type."

Those friendly blue eyes took on a little edge, and she tipped her face up, facing off with him boldly as he stepped even closer until he almost had her pinned against the tile wall.

"And what type would that be?" he asked, his voice low so only she could hear.

She craned her neck to look past his shoulder. "Randi will be back out any second. I wonder how she's doing."

Travis only extended one arm, planting his hand on the wall aside of her, leaning in.

"I'm sure they're fine. What type of man do you want, Penny? I'm sure we could work something out."

Penny inhaled sharply, which was a totally stupid thing to do because even in the antiseptic atmosphere of the hospital ward, Travis's fresh, clean scent was heavenly.

"Back off, will ya?" She pushed forward, planting her hands on his shoulder, only to have him pull her up close, sliding a look from side to side to make sure they were alone. Then, before she could wrestle free, he swooped in and covered her mouth with his, one fast, hot kiss that shot heat straight to all the places that counted. Places that hadn't received much attention lately.

He let his mouth linger on hers for a minute, then he backed away slowly, satisfied as he took in her flushed cheeks and dazed eyes. The night-duty nurse clattered down the hall with the medicine tray, rolling along in between them, but even that didn't break the spell.

"Just something for you to think about, in case you decide I might be your type after all."

Travis winked and turned to walk down the hall.

Penny ground her teeth, berating herself mentally for melting from one hot kiss. She would just have to make sure that *that* never happened again.

FOR A MOMENT Miranda stood by the door watching Colin sleep. He looked so different from the vibrant man whom she had tried to seduce a few hours earlier. Embarrassment flowed though her as she recalled the disaster *that* had been. Well, Travis said Colin had lost his memory, so she could only hope and pray he didn't remember.

She took another step forward, and then another, swallowing visibly as she saw how pale he was. Her heart constricted as she surveyed the purple bruises on his face and arms. Tears threatened again. Biting her lip hard, she reminded herself that he was fine. Travis said he was fine.

She didn't want to wake him though she wanted to know what his response to her would be. Free to stare, to observe the angles of his face, the texture of his skin, she watched him, thankful that he was still here with her. What had happened between them almost didn't matter, compared to this. Nothing mattered as long as he was all right.

Sighing, she figured she should leave. Tomorrow would come soon enough, and she would help in whatever ways she could. There was no reason for Ed and Joyce to miss their anniversary trip. Her work schedule was flexible, and she could reschedule appointments if need be to help out Colin.

Reaching forward, she smiled slightly and ran the back of her finger over Colin's cheek.

"I'll be back to see you tomorrow, big guy."

When she turned to go, she heard a grunt and a croaking noise. Glancing back, she saw Colin's eyes flutter open and her heart leaped. He focused in on her, his eyes heavy from the sedation, and she returned to the bedside.

"Hey there."

"Randi?" His voice was a grating whisper, but it was enough to make her heart pound with relief.

"You remember me."

His chuckle came out as a rasp. She smiled and touched his forehead but drew her hand back almost as quickly as she had extended it.

"Let me get you some water." She poured water from the pitcher on the stand and leaned forward, cradling his head while tipping the cup slightly forward with the other.

"Better?"

He nodded and winced as she removed her hand.

"Listen, I'll come by tomorrow morning. You rest now."

Bleary hazel eyes blinked again and watched her closely.

"I can't remember…what happened. The last thing I remember was getting an e-mail from you earlier today…do you know what I was doing out there tonight? Was I with you?"

Unsure of what to say, she smiled brightly and patted his hand, anxious to leave.

"Don't worry about it. We can talk tomorrow."

"But—"

She cut him off in a playfully stern voice. "You need to sleep, or Travis will have both our heads. See you tomorrow."

She walked away from the bed and sighed in relief, but it was only momentary. Who knew what the morning would bring?

TWO BOTTLES OF WINE and several hours later, Penny and Miranda were sprawled across Miranda's couch, exhausted and depressed from the events of the day. Miranda told the story of her failed seduction, and Penny squirmed as she told the tale of Travis's kiss—both were at their wit's end about how to handle their respective situations.

Miranda lolled her head over against a pillow and sighed. Penny's problems were solved for the moment, and she was snoring like a lumberjack. No wonder. They had finished the champagne she had put out for Colin and then opened a good merlot and drunk that.

She looked at her watch. Two in the morning. Great. Definitely time for bed, or she would not make it to the hospital at all in the morning. Standing on wobbly knees, she leaned over and grabbed Penny's ankles, stretching her out on the sofa and ignoring the nonsensical mumblings Penny was making. Then Miranda grabbed a blanket and threw it over her, face and all.

Satisfied that Penny was well tucked in, she glanced at the two empty bottles on the table and shrugged.

Staring harder, she cocked her head sideways, noticing that the bottles were on top of the magazine that had given her the idea for that stupid seduction in the first place. While picking it up, one of the empty bottles rolled to the floor. She stuck her tongue out at the magazine and then winged it clear across the room with a few choice words flung after it.

Stumbling forward, she hit her toe on the edge of the coffee table. Damn, this just wasn't her night. Hobbling, she headed toward the stairs and her room. She would have to set her alarm to wake up Penny in time for work. Only five hours from now. That sucked.

Everything sucked. She was crazy about Colin, and he wasn't in the least interested in her. How the heck had he ended up falling into the harbor after he left her? Now he had amnesia and, with her luck, he would remember everything by morning, and she would resume her full-fledged-idiot status. And her toe hurt, which probably was going to match what her head would feel like in the morning. Just great. She wished *she* could forget all this. Colin was lucky.

She walked to the back door and whistled. Lucy and Chuck came bounding around the corner and ran outside for their nightly business. Lucy was a medium sized pit bull/Lab mix she had rescued from the shelter when she moved here. Miranda had found Chuck, an indolent basset hound with irresistible ears and woeful brown eyes, in Denver. Miranda loved them both, and would get more pets if she had the room. Calling them back in, she pointed up the stairs, and they ran to their beds in the corner of her room.

Turning on the landing and following the dogs upstairs, she yawned and wondered if Colin really would remember. As much as she wanted him to be okay, it would be nice if her little snafu never made it to the light of his consciousness again. Really, in the scope of things, what was a few lost hours?

What if he didn't *ever* remember? Travis said sometimes it was permanent, right?

A bad plan started forming at the edges of her thoughts. She knew it was bad because, well, she just had that feeling, the same feeling she'd had when she tried the old I'm-gonna-seduce-Colin routine. Peeling off her clothes, she didn't even bother putting on pajamas. She just crawled under the covers, forgetting the alarm clock altogether.

Instead of passing out as Penny had been so fortunate to do, her mind kept spinning, trying to work out that vague idea forming on the alcohol-fuzzed horizon.

If Colin never remembered what had happened last night, could she tell him whatever she wished had happened? Could she rewrite history a little—well, okay, a lot—just for those few hours? Then she could finally make him see that they belonged together as more than friends.

It would be wrong...but only a little, right?

After all, it was clear that he had wanted her as much as she wanted him. He was held back by some misguided idea that she was replacing Derek with him.

What if this little amnesia thing was her opportunity to remove that roadblock? Practically humming with possibility, and in spite of her better judgment, her mind continued to spin out a plan until the wine finally took its toll and she fell asleep.

4

COLIN REACHED OUT, not understanding how or why he was suddenly standing here looking at Miranda, who was smiling coyly as she half lay on the bed. Her beautiful naked form was draped in a cream-colored satin lace nightgown. Because everything around her was gauzy, like in an airbrushed photograph, he knew he must be dreaming. It did smell funny, though. Instead of perfume and flowers, the dream had a more antiseptic odor that had him wriggling his nose, but he shrugged. Who cared about that when Miranda was gazing at him seductively, his for the taking?

And at least in his dreams, he could take her. He had hot dreams about Miranda fairly frequently, and the strange odor, whatever it was, wasn't enough to stop him. He took a step forward and slid his fingers underneath the flimsy shoulder strap of the lace nightgown, easing it over her slim shoulders. Her head fell back and she moaned, sending a wave of desire pulsing through him. He kissed her deeply, letting himself go; hell, it was his dream, he might as well indulge. Her lips were like silk and he knew he needed to be inside of her.

Magically, he was suddenly naked. He loved that about dreams, just think it and it became real.

He had pushed her soft thighs apart, preparing to settle himself into ecstasy, when he suddenly found himself looking at his own image in a mirror he was standing in front of. Miranda was kneeling before him. His hands were wrapped in her hair as she dragged her tongue up his thigh, the sharp nip of her teeth startling him in the best possible way before she slid those luscious lips over his cock, taking him completely, and his world tilted sideways. This could potentially be the best dream he'd *ever* had.

She suckled him, closing her amazingly strong hands over his butt cheeks, squeezing and murmuring unintelligible things against his skin. Pleasure shot through him and he was surprised he could even continue standing. Watching her kiss him so intimately, he groaned. It wasn't what he'd originally had in mind, but he wasn't about to argue as she let him sink deeply into her hot mouth, encompassing him to the hilt over and over until sweet release started to build. Then his focus was shattered by a screamingly bright light that seemed to shine out of the mirror. He fought desperately to hold on to the pulsing pleasure, but consciousness encroached and he groaned, frustrated by the interruption.

"Colin, hey, whoa, that's some dream you must be having, but let's wake up now, okay?"

That definitely was *not* Miranda's voice. Colin tried to focus back on Miranda, but she was fading away, slipping from him as reality and the throbbing pain in his head set in. Opening his eyes, he started when he met Travis's eyes, up close and personal. Travis bent close, opening one eyelid then the other, shining a light that just increased the stabbing pain he was already feeling, then proceeded to check his other vitals without saying a word.

"Some parts of you are quite alert this morning apparently...would it be inappropriate for me to inquire how you're feeling?"

Colin realized his dream-induced erection hadn't quite faded with the dream. He could only be grateful now he hadn't reached climax or he would have really been embarrassed. Looking up at Travis and twisting his face away from the probing light, he growled.

"I feel like shit."

"That sounds about right. The meds are wearing off. You'll be logy for a while, but then things will clear up. We'll give you some painkillers for the aches, but nothing too strong—you need to get back on your feet today."

"I can't feel my feet. Wait, yes, I can, and they hurt. Everything hurts."

Travis grinned down at him, sticking his hands into his pockets. "Aw, quit your whining. You were lucky— could have been much worse."

"How the hell did I end up here with you poking and prodding at me?"

Travis shrugged and wrote something on his chart before answering.

"So you don't remember our talk from last night?

Do you remember anything else? Your mom and dad coming in, Miranda?"

Colin's attention perked. "Miranda was here?"

Travis nodded and made another note. "Don't worry too much about it. Memory lapses are common with this kind of thing. What's important is that you made it out all in one piece." Travis's eyes turned serious when he stopped writing. "Seriously, Col, you were lucky. It may not feel like it at the moment, but if you'd been in the water any longer, things would have been a lot worse."

Colin raised his eyebrows and winced. "I fell in the water? Lord. I can't remember anything. When will my memory come back?"

"Hard to say. Amnesia can be temporary, but sometimes people will permanently lose their memories of the time surrounding a traumatic incident. You might also have a little trouble with your immediate memory in the next few days, forgetting where you put your coffee or your keys. It's normal."

Colin furrowed his brow, concentrating, but all he could recall of the preceding day was correcting papers and getting an e-mail from Miranda. Travis reached over and patted his shoulder companionably.

"Don't force it. If it comes, it comes. You probably stopped for a beer, went for a walk and didn't see those bikes coming."

"Bikes?"

"You were knocked over the rail by a bicyclist. We talked about that a little last night, but you were pretty out of it."

"Did anyone else get hurt?"

"Just minor injuries. You were kind enough to block one guy's fall and prevent him from pitching over the side. Other than that, they didn't have much to add, just that you were standing there and then suddenly you turned into their path." Travis adjusted something on Colin's IV, then continued.

"They tried to avoid you, but it was too late. The one who was left standing called the rescue unit and sent up a flare, flagging in a nearby boat with his emergency flashlight." Travis grinned. "I'll never make fun of yuppies who get all geared up for a ride through the city again. He saved your life."

Colin blinked, the enormity of the situation settling in. He had fallen, could've died—and he didn't remember any of it. It was extraordinarily frustrating. And surreal. Waking up the hospital and having no idea why was one of the most disturbing experiences he'd ever had. As a psychologist he had always wondered what amnesia would feel like. Basically, it sucked.

In spite of Travis's casual response, it was unnerving to know something had happened and not be able to remember what it was. Exhaustion was starting to replace frustration, but he forced himself to stay awake.

"When am I out of here?"

"Later today. Your vitals are fine. We'll get you up and walking, see how you do, then your mom said she and your dad would come get you. You're staying with them for the night."

Colin eyed Travis's amused expression warily.

"Is that really necessary?"

"Probably not, but I told her it was a great idea, because it was fun to think of you being fed green Jell-O and tucked away in front of the TV in your jammies."

"That's just great. Thanks a bunch."

"No problem. But seriously, Col, it wouldn't hurt for you to have someone around for your first night home, and it will make them feel better, too. Randi and I talked them out of canceling their trip, so you are only hostage for one night. Enjoy it."

Colin smirked and let his head fall back on the pillow before his tone turned serious again.

"They were okay?"

"They were scared, but they know you're okay, and I'm sure they'll be here soon."

"I have to call the university. When can I get back to work?"

"We called them to report your accident, but you can go back as soon as you feel up to it. Give it until tomorrow, at least, but then it's up to you. I've gotta go finish my rounds." He pushed the phone closer to the bed. "Oh, and not that I care to see you naked again, but you'll need to schedule a follow-up in three to five days. Routine. And call immediately if anything gets worse or seems wrong."

Colin nodded, and Travis headed toward the door. "See you later, bud. A nurse will be in shortly to help you out. Don't try getting out of bed on your own, or you'll embarrass yourself. Maybe I'll stop by tonight for some Jell-O."

MIRANDA LOOKED AT THE young couple sitting across from her, their three-month-old Lab puppy squirming in the wife's lap. She loved all dogs, and Lab puppies were especially irresistible. Their big brown eyes got her every time, but she knew they could also be completely unmanageable if they weren't properly trained, and that was the case now.

"You have to change your behavior, too. It's not just about training the puppy. But with some work, she'll be a great joy to both of you."

Apparently the pup's behavior was fast becoming a marital issue between the couple. The husband, Phil, had made the appointment for training, threatening to get rid of the pup if they didn't attend. Miranda knew she had to do a little convincing here, especially for Mindy, Phil's wife. Mindy hugged the Lab protectively, convinced training might traumatize her "baby," staring at the toothed training collar as if it was a torture device.

"Watch, Mindy, you'll see this collar doesn't really hurt at all, used correctly." Miranda put the collar around her upper arm and pulled. The couple peered at each other uncertainly. Miranda took the collar off her arm. "See? No damage, just a pinching. The collar mimics the mother dog's nip when she disciplines them. You don't drag or yank the collar too hard, you just give it a pull. Will you let me have Precious so I can show you?"

Mindy reluctantly handed over the puppy at her husband's urging. Miranda fought a grimace. It was too cute a puppy to have such a totally ridiculous name, but that was life. She'd heard much worse.

She put the pup on the floor, clasped the collar around its neck and then just walked away. The pup didn't follow, so Miranda gave the collar a sharp tug from the leash, never looking back. Precious let out a yelp, followed quickly by a yelp from Mindy, who stayed in her chair, nonetheless. The startled puppy learned quickly and, after a second tug, was obediently following along. She had to walk in some pretty tight circles—the office space was tiny. She had just enough room for her desk and kept the rest clear for working with the dogs. If business picked up, she definitely would need larger digs.

"See, this is all you have to do. Just a few minutes a few times each day. Don't take her to public places until you check with your vet to make sure she is protected and has all her shots. Pups are susceptible to some nasty diseases."

Miranda stopped in front of Mindy. "Here, now you and Phil try, and make sure she stays at your feet—she doesn't decide where to go, you do. That's the rule. Change directions frequently so you are leading her and not vice versa."

Mindy apprehensively took the leash, but soon broke out into a huge smile and laughed in delight when the puppy happily followed along. Miranda smiled, too. The pup was a smart one and was training fast. She felt confident that she might be able to make a success of this after all.

She'd had her doubts. Doing volunteer training and

taking responsibility for your own business were two very different things. But she'd learned more than she thought through her previous experience, and she would be linking up with some local groups to undertake more advanced training. She also enjoyed teaching the people as much as the dogs, which she'd been nervous about. Miranda watched the young couple interact with their puppy and felt a sense of pride in her work. She was excited by her current successes, small as they may be, and her plans for the future.

"Just keep doing this each day, but not too long at one time, since it's very tiring for pups to focus on their lessons. I'll see you next week?"

Mindy looked at her, now full of enthusiasm. "Oh, yes! We'll be here! And I am going to tell all my friends with dogs about you!"

Miranda smiled at the praise. "That is always appreciated." As Phil and Mindy started out the door, Miranda reminded them one more time, "Make sure you go through the door before her. Don't let her lead you!"

She laughed as they tried to fit back through the door and got all jumbled up. They'd get there. They loved their dog and were willing to work at it, and that was key. Hard work and love and the ability to adapt were probably the basics of all relationships. That awareness led her to other thoughts, notably ones about her situation with Colin.

Slumping back in her chair, she leaned over the side to retrieve a yogurt, water and an apple from her small office refrigerator. She was happy with how the morning's work had gone, but she was also exhausted and more than a little hungover. It was time for more aspirin. She'd woken up late, almost forgetting this early appointment and had rushed out the door. She'd left Penny, who had somehow ended up on the floor with the dogs, sleeping.

Chomping her apple and feeling her empty tum gurgle in appreciation for some healthy food, she dug into her bag and pulled out the magazine, now torn and dirty but still readable. She should throw it out. But then again, if she was seriously thinking of seeing this seduction scenario through, she needed some ideas. Flipping the pages, she found the article again. She read the outline of the steps, thinking they made a lot of sense.

1) Energize: Take control, be the seductress, and take the pressure off of the man in your life.

2) Experiment: Engage in a sexual adventure that is new for both of you.

3) Explore: Go away somewhere new for a romantic weekend.

4) Embrace: Share and submit to each other's secret fantasies.

5) Expose: Spend an evening naked in body and soul—share your hidden secrets.

Her mind started to perk with possibilities as she read the third step. Get away to a new place. The article said that just being together in a new location was sexually stimulating for many couples, so they should find time to spend a weekend away, someplace they both would enjoy.

The last two steps had her intrigued and a little worried. The plan was to build intimacy and encourage sexual fun, so these steps required sharing as well as daring.

Well, if they got through the first four, it would be a certified miracle. She set the magazine back on the desk, biting into her apple and trying to mute the annoying little voice in her head that suggested her plan was not entirely fair, that she was taking advantage of Colin's loss of memory, capitalizing on a weakness.

The other, more stubborn side argued that perhaps fate had intervened and she would be a fool not to try. She had feelings for him, not that she knew exactly what those feelings were, but she wanted to find out. From what she could tell of his response to her, he wanted her, too. She was just going to give things a little push. However, she couldn't do any of it until she got home and took a shower so she didn't smell like a dog. Then she would see about setting her plan into motion.

MIRANDA PULLED UP in front of Colin's home and paused for a few moments before opening her car door. The ten-minute drive from the city hadn't relaxed her at all, and after she had approached the door and knocked, she almost decided to turn around and leave. However, since the door was open, she stuck her head in and shouted, "Anyone home?"

"In here." The voice came from the living room and she headed in that direction. She'd already made the decision, and she wasn't backing down now. Walking down the narrow hallway of the old house to the living room, she spotted Colin sitting in the old burgundy leather recliner that had been his father's.

Miranda smiled, recalling that when Joyce had threatened to put it at the curb for garbage collection, Colin had jumped at the chance to put the comfortable old chair in his own home. And his father still got to use it when they took in a game.

When she reached Colin's side, she bent to grace his cheek with a kiss. Then she drew back and looked into his face, studying the bruises that looked even larger than they had the night before.

"It looks worse than it feels, most the time."

"I thought you would be at your mom's."

Colin waved his hand dismissively. "Nah. I'm a little old to be tucked in, and I felt better coming back here. Besides, they're going crazy trying to get ready for their trip, and my mom has been here constantly, bringing food, making sure I'm all right. It's a blessing and a curse having them live just a few miles away. I'm glad they didn't cancel their trip."

"They leave tomorrow?"

"As planned. It will be good for them. And for me. I have so much food in there you all will have to come over and help me out with it."

"No problem there." Joyce was a fantastic cook, and Miranda never turned down good food. "Anyway, I wanted to come by and see how things were, but we also need to talk about something."

She stretched an arm over the coffee table that was between them and grasped his hand, watching his eyebrows quirk at the gesture. "About last night...I know you wanted to know what happened." Her stomach did a little crazy flip when she saw the eagerness in his eyes.

"Please, anything you can tell me might trigger my memory."

"Well, remember in my e-mail I invited you over and told you not to say anything?"

His brow furrowed, and he nodded. His eyes flitted down to their joined hands. He suddenly seemed less comfortable and shifted in his chair a little. "Yeah, what was that about?"

She tried to sound casual, but her voice shook even though this part of her story was absolutely true. "Well...I invited you over because I intended to seduce you. And I did."

Silence hung between them for another moment.

"You what?" He repeated his question in a hoarse whisper, staring at her as if she'd lost her mind.

Miranda closed her eyes and searched for courage. Was it so unbelievable to him that she had seduced him? Yeah, it probably was.

"I wanted to seduce you—and I did."

Colin appeared to be literally shocked speechless. When he found his voice, his tone reflected his state of disbelief.

"I don't believe it. I'd have remembered *that*. Is this a joke Travis put you up to? Is he hiding outside the window, the sick bastard?" Colin half grinned and stretched to look out the window, wincing again with the effort.

Miranda swallowed deeply and continued. "You were surprised at first, of course, but I figured you would be. That's why I didn't want you to speak. I wanted to give us a chance. Then I fed you strawberries and champagne, I undressed you, then I…I, um, stripped for you, then we had sex. Made love…we made love. We're lovers, Colin."

There, it was out. She waited as Colin sat stock-still, with a stunned expression. He shook his head.

"You're not kidding? Why would you do that?"

"Because I wanted you. I've always wanted you and it's been driving me crazy. And because, from what I could tell from your response, you want me, too. After my accident in Denver, I just learned not to let things go. You have to go after what you want. And I wanted you."

He didn't respond, but looked away as if processing the information. Miranda held her tongue. The ball was in his court. He turned back to her, his eyes guarded.

"Um, what did you wear last night?"

The question caught her off guard and she blinked. "Huh?"

"You said you seduced me. Did you wear anything special?"

"Um, yeah. A see-through lace nightgown."

"It was off-white? With thin straps and long slits up the side?"

She nodded slowly, holding her breath. Had she jiggled his memory loose?

Colin sat back, looking dazed. "I guess you must be right. I dreamed about you in that gown last night. I thought it was the drugs they gave me. Um, was there a mirror involved by any chance?" She nodded mutely, and he looked more than a little uncomfortable when he continued. "I guess it wasn't a dream. It must have been a memory, because that's what you were wearing in my dream. That gown. I remembered it. And the mirror. I think I remembered…touching you."

He sounded awed and confused. She got up and crossed to him, sitting on the edge of the chair, leaning forward until her face was close to his, and spoke gently.

"I'm glad you remembered that."

"I'm not so sure I am."

She pulled back, going still.

"What do you mean?"

He was quiet, and she held her breath. When he looked at her, she felt the impact of the emotions—desire, confusion, and other things she couldn't name—in his eyes. When he spoke, his voice reflected all of it.

"If I told you I didn't want you that would be a lie. I guess you know that now. But I wish I could remember more. What else happened? What was I doing out in Old Port instead of with you if we were, um, together?"

Colin watched Miranda's body language and facial expression tense. Clearly, there was more to the story.

"Well, we had an argument."

"We slept together and then argued?" At the oddness, he almost laughed. Wasn't it usually the other way around with most couples? "What did we fight about?"

"Well, we were caught up in the moment, and then afterward you had some misgivings and said you wanted to go, that you had to think. We argued because, well, I hated that you regretted being with me. But you left. Then I heard you were hurt, and I…well…all I could think was that—" Her eyes filled as she remembered Travis's phone call, and she turned away, not wanting Colin to know how frightened she had been.

"Hey, I'm okay. I promise." He put his arms around her as if it were the most natural thing in the world, and rubbed his cheek on her hair. Colin couldn't remember what he had done or felt the night before, but right now he was feeling confused and…aroused. Most definitely aroused—Lord, she was so soft. Even in his dreams he never could imagine how soft she was.

He didn't know exactly how to handle the news she had given him, but he apparently had handled it badly last night. It must have hurt her for him to leave after they had made love. His frustration rose to a new pitch. He'd made love with Miranda, and he couldn't even remember it. He wished even harder for those hours to return to his memory and that he could take his foolish actions back. Though he wasn't sure which was more foolish, giving in to his desire for her, or leaving her after he had.

He wanted her, so much so that he was in more pain from that than from his fall. She smelled so good, so sweet and musky, it was overtaking his senses as he lost himself in the silky slide of her hair against his skin. He'd dreamed of this, of holding her close, for what seemed like forever. Apparently he wasn't as strong as he had thought. He should never have slept with her, but now that he had, even though he couldn't remember, all the well-constructed emotional fencing he had built between them felt as if it had been ripped away.

In fact, knowing now that he had been with her, but had lost the memory, seemed to intensify the need that was quickly building within him. Suddenly it didn't matter if he would always be second-best to Derek, if she was just using him to work through her issues. All that mattered was that she was with him, in his arms, and his body was hard as iron. He had to have her. He wanted to lose himself in her and forget everything else.

He slid his palm along her cheek, reveling in its smoothness, in being able to touch her as he had always dreamed of. Threading his hand into the curtain of hair that fell over her shoulder, he pulled her even closer. She looked at him quietly, her eyes still damp.

"Col?"

"Shh. No talk."

He pressed his mouth to hers. Every ache, every pain practically disappeared as her warm mouth opened eagerly under his. All he could think of was that he wanted more, that he wanted her naked, now, and as close to him as a man and woman could get. He was tired of settling for dreams.

Though he was reeling with the sensations of actually kissing Miranda, the hot way her tongue was curling around his and how she was nipping at his lower lip, something in the back of his mind kept tugging at his consciousness, tainting the moment.

But he wasn't going to let anything interrupt this, and he pushed any doubts back, ignoring them completely. He wanted a moment with Miranda that he could remember. And she was feeling it, too, moaning against his mouth in ways beyond the boundaries of anything he had ever imagined.

The kiss was turning quickly into much more, his hands finding their way around her body as if they had done so a million times, yet every discovery was fresh and new. Maybe amnesia wasn't so bad after all. She groaned, sliding her hands inside of his shirt and gently touching him.

He knew she was being careful, trying not to hurt him, but he pulled her hard against him. He didn't care if it hurt. He wanted every sensation possible as long as it came from her body moving against his. He wanted her hands on him as they were now, her nails scraping lightly against his back, moving slowly lower until he growled his need against her mouth. He had to have her. Now.

MIRANDA'S BREATH WAS coming in short pants, and she could barely think straight. She was sitting here getting hot and heavy with Colin, the man she wanted above all others, the man she had orchestrated a great lie to seduce, but while her skin was alive with wanting him, she felt a heavy reluctance pulling at her heart. She wanted him, but did she want him like this?

A massive avalanche of doubts about her plan to seduce Colin toppled down on her, even as his wonderfully skilled lips nibbled at her neck, sending sharp arrows of pleasure shooting through her body. What had she been thinking? She was playing a dangerous game here.

Colin could have died, and she was taking advantage of the situation. Shame made her stomach queasy. She pulled away, stepping back, shaking her head to clear her muddled thoughts. Colin pinned her with a look that seemed to see right into her deepest places. She stood, frozen by his stare, and backed out of the room, unable to say anything. She heard more than saw him get up and follow her.

As she walked to the door, she knew Colin was right behind her.

"Miranda."

Stepping out into the cool evening air, she stopped but didn't turn to face him. She shivered, the cool breeze flitting over her hot, aroused skin. What now? What could she possibly say?

When he stepped up behind her, so close that his scent surrounded her she held her breath. He closed a firm hand over her shoulder, his breath feathering by her ear when he spoke.

"What happened in there? Why did you pull away from me?"

She shrugged, shook her head, unable to face him. She was torn and miserable—she wanted him so much, but to tell him the truth meant she would lose any chance of having him. Words lodged, frozen in her throat. She'd really done it this time.

His hand on her shoulder applied gentle pressure and he turned her around to face him, his eyes glittering down at her. In the darkness he seemed taller than usual, making her feel almost dwarfed, an unusual experience for her. The heat from his body so close to hers warmed her and desire twisted her from the inside out.

"Tell me what happened in there."

"I'm sorry, Colin." She sighed, not quite knowing what to say. "I just…I know you just got out of the hospital, and I shouldn't be dumping all this on you, and I shouldn't have…." The words came out on a whoosh of air as she released the breath that had been a tight knot in her chest. She didn't stop him when he pulled her closer, wrapping his arms around her loosely. She put her hands on his stomach, lightly, tentatively, feeling wrong and oh-so-right at the same time.

Groaning at the mess she had created, she dropped her forehead to his shoulder and berated herself silently. Then she felt the brush of his mouth on her cheek, the light scrape of his beard on her skin, and her heart sang in response. She wanted this sooooo much. Wanted him. But it wasn't real—he was only acting this way because of what she'd told him.

Pulling back from him, she took a deep breath and shoved her hands in her pockets.

"Colin, we have to talk."

He was quiet, watching her closely, and nodded.

"I know. Even though I don't remember much, I can feel how things have changed between us."

Her heart dropped down into her knees. Maybe it didn't matter if she'd lied or not. He'd only lost a few hours, but all of the memories of Derek, all of the reasons he wouldn't be with her before, remained. She'd been foolish to think she could change that. She was so caught up in her crazy plan she hadn't really thought the situation through. She barely realized he had stepped closer again, was speaking to her.

"I don't know if I'll ever remember what happened between us, Miranda, but I hope I will. Especially if it was the beginning of something I've wanted but didn't think we could have."

He reached down, taking her hand in his, stroking the top of her hand with his thumb, creating maddening swirls of pleasure that radiated throughout her body.

"But I guess we can always make a new beginning for ourselves, right? When you came home a few months ago, when I saw you, you said your accident had made you reassess life, made you less worried about the small stuff. I think I've been too worried about the small stuff. Ego, the past. I let it get in between us."

His voice was soft and suggestive, and she could hardly believe he was standing here, speaking to her in those sexy, hopeful tones. What he was saying settled in. He'd wanted her before. He had just been too reluctant to do anything about it, and now he wasn't. He *wanted* a new beginning with her. Did it matter how they got there if the end result was both of them finally being happy? Confused by her thoughts, reined in by her conscience, she retreated but didn't release his hand.

"I think it would be good for us to take a breather and think about it, talk a little, before we do anything rash."

A little too late for that, don't you think? the small voice inside her mind mocked her.

Colin squeezed her hand, and she gazed into his face, struck once more by how handsome he was in the muted evening light, even with his bruises. His sandy hair was mussed, as usual, and he looked tired, but it didn't affect how simply seeing him, standing close to him made her heart race. He was looking down at her so intently, the shadow of his beard added a kind of sexy earthiness that had her hormones on overdrive.

Don't do anything rash? Right. For a split second she considered throwing herself at him and doing whatever they could manage right there on his front stoop. But he stepped back and let go of her hand. She nearly whimpered at the loss of contact. God, she was a mess.

"Listen, it's been a rough day. I have to admit I'm still working this out, and not being able to remember is driving me crazy. But I want you to know I'm here, and I'm not running away, like I apparently did last night. I'm sorry for that. I really am. I can't believe I left you like that. I won't do it again."

Miranda looked down at her feet, jamming her toe into the paved walk. It was official. She was a bad person, letting him believe he had done something wrong the night before. But even so she couldn't seem to choke up the words about what really happened. Instead, she decided to downplay it.

"It wasn't *that* bad. I understand why you needed to go. Let's forget it." She winced immediately, regretting her poor choice of words, but he smiled and then actually laughed. What a great laugh.

"I guess I have that part covered, anyway."

She smiled, backing away.

"Um, I have to go. I have to get the dogs. It's getting late and I left them at Mom's."

"Why didn't you bring them?"

"I didn't know how you'd be feeling, and anyway, they like visiting her. She gives them treats and lets them get away with being naughty."

"Okay. Tell her I said hi. I'll, um, talk to you tomorrow?"

She walked backward, stepping away slowly in the opposite direction.

"Sure, yeah, I'll come by to see how you are. Or, you know, you call me, if you need anything."

He nodded, and she turned around and headed to her car, wondering what tomorrow was going to bring and how she was going to deal with it.

5

MIRANDA DROVE a mile down the road from Colin's home to the house where she had grown up. Her mind was a whirl of activity, her body still aching from Colin's touch and from walking away from him. If she had stayed, no doubt they would be in bed right now with him thrusting deeply inside of her. The thought made her reflexively clench her thighs together, and she sighed, unsure of what to do or what to feel.

She sat outside in the car for a while, trying to get hold of herself, refocusing on the old neighborhood. There had been changes. The area was getting more and more developed—they actually had streetlights now. When she was growing up, it had been more rural and there were no sidewalks or streetlights. She'd gotten to her friends' houses then by crossing fields and woods. But now it was looking more and more like most suburbs. She got out of the car and inhaled the air. That hadn't changed, and the surrounding pine woods still scented the yard and welcomed her home. Likewise, the screen door still scraped the porch floor when she yanked it open. The familiar sound brought comfort.

"Mom?"

"In here."

Miranda heard nails scratching on the hardwood floors and was suddenly overcome with doggy welcomes as Chuck and Lucy bounded to the door, vying for as much attention as they could get. She gave them both enthusiastic greetings and then made her way into the living room where her mother sat reading.

"Where's Dad?"

"He's gone to D.C., remember? On business. I hate it when he's gone. The house is too quiet, so these two are especially welcome." She smiled at her "grandpuppies" as they returned to curl up on her feet.

"I can leave them here tonight if you want."

"Oh, that's not necessary, unless you have plans? How are the Jacobs?"

"I only saw them for a minute. Colin wasn't staying there—he was at his own house."

"So soon? Wasn't he just released?"

"Yeah, but he was in pretty good shape." Remembering his hands on her skin, she wrapped her arms around herself as she felt her nipples bud against her blouse. "He's just nursing some bumps and bruises."

"Joyce said he had amnesia?"

"Yeah, but it's minor. He lost a few hours on the night of the accident. They figure it'll come back on its own."

"Still, that must be frightening, to not know what happened in your life, even for a few hours."

"He's handling it well. He was pretty lucky."

Dee nodded. "Gives you two something in common, I guess. Still gives me shudders when I think about what could have happened to you."

"I know. Me, too. But I'm fine now. So is Colin."

"I would have sent something, but I know they're leaving tomorrow, and knowing Joyce, she probably baked her nerves away all day. She's been so excited about this trip. I take it they're still going?"

"Yeah, tomorrow." Miranda sank down on the old sofa across from her mother.

"What are you reading?"

"A mystery. It's the latest in this series, you know, the one with the bounty hunters I was telling you about. I've been dying to find out what happens. With your Dad out of town, I've got time to catch up on my reading."

"That's looking on the bright side." Miranda smiled and looked at the book. "You gave me the first one, and I keep meaning to get to it."

Her mother assessed Miranda quickly with sharp brown eyes that matched her daughter's, and set the book in her lap.

"So, what's wrong?"

Miranda's eyes widened innocently. "What do you mean? Nothing's wrong."

Dee Carter took her reading glasses off and leveled a look at her daughter, crossing her arms over her waist, humor and concern reflected in her expression.

"Miranda. You're not one much for small talk, but ever since you were little, when you had a problem you would always come sit down with me and ask questions about what I was doing, or how was work—so, what's wrong?"

Miranda groaned, knowing her mother was absolutely right. But still. "A daughter can't have an interest in her mother's life?"

"Of course, and I appreciate you asking. You're a wonderful and considerate girl." Dee's eyes twinkled. "What's on your mind?"

Miranda picked at some lint on a blanket that was thrown over the back of the couch.

"Okay. I think I screwed something up."

"At work?"

She shook her head. "With Colin. I, um…well, Col has this thing about me and Derek, like I am still his girlfriend or something. It bugs me."

Dee looked taken aback. "Why would it? You *were* Derek's girlfriend, if only for that short time."

Miranda got up from her seat and paced across the room. "See, that's just it! It was just a couple months. We weren't in love or anything. But everyone acts as if we were."

Her mother was silent for a few moments.

"Are you positive it's Colin who has the problem holding on to his brother's memory? It sounds as though you have something you've been holding on to as well."

Miranda stood in the doorway of the dining room, wringing her hands.

"Yeah, sort of. I…what would you think if I told you Derek and I weren't actually dating when he was killed?"

Dee shrugged a little. "Really? Why wouldn't you have told us that?"

Crossing back to the sofa, Miranda sat down, suddenly needing someone to know, someone other than Penny. "I couldn't. We'd just broken up a few hours before his accident."

"Oh, honey!" Miranda saw understanding and surprise dawn on her mother's features. "Was Derek that upset about the breakup? Do you think that was your fault?" Dee slid across the couch and wrapped an arm around her daughter's shoulders, giving her a squeeze, then settled back. Miranda hurried to explain.

"No. No, nothing like that. That's what I mean. He wasn't upset at all. We weren't really that close, we just had some fun together. There wasn't any, you know, spark, there. We were just friends. I mean, we, uh, kissed and stuff, you know—"

Her mother nodded in understanding. "No need for details, dear. There are some things a mother doesn't need to hear. I don't remember it all very well, but I guess I can see how you might have felt awkward telling people you broke up with him, but how does that matter now?"

Miranda was suddenly choked by tears. She was tired and her emotions had been running high for too many hours, making it hard to talk. "I...I thought Colin, and his family, would bl-blame me, you know, that I upset him, and then he had his accident...." She sniffed, trying to choke back her tears. Her mother moved over again, hugging her close.

"Oh, baby. They would never do that, even if Derek had been upset. How could you have had such an idea in your head all this time? Derek's accident was one of those horrible freak things."

Miranda sighed. "The only one who knows is Penny, because she knew we were breaking up before we actually did. After the accident, I couldn't bear to tell anyone."

"And this involves Colin how…?"

Miranda felt her face warm and wasn't quite sure how to go about this part of the conversation. She really didn't want to tell her mom about Colin and what she had done, but she was so confused at the moment.

"Ahh, I see."

Miranda looked up sharply. "What?"

Dee smiled gently. "You know, I always wondered about you two. You and Colin. You always seemed… I don't know, partial to him. He's the only one you would share your ice cream with when you were little." She chuckled lightly at the memory. "I remember actually being rather surprised when you went out with Derek, but then again, who can know what's going on in a teenage girl's head?"

Or in a twenty-eight-year-old girl's head, Miranda thought wryly to herself. Her mother was far too perceptive.

"Yeah, well. Colin's never seemed to have much interest in me."

Her frustration must have come through her voice.

"And you have feelings for Colin? And he doesn't for you?"

Miranda screwed her mouth to the side. "Something like that."

Dee sat back, appearing to consider her daughter's situation, and finally spoke.

"Well, it seems that if you have feelings for Colin, and you want to let him know you didn't have anything serious with Derek, you need to tell him that. Get things out in the open."

Miranda rubbed her palms on the thighs of her jeans. If only it were that easy. After the whopper she had told Colin tonight, getting things out in the open had taken on a whole new meaning.

"Yeah, that's a thought. Thanks, Mom."

"How serious are these feelings?"

"I don't know. I have to think about it."

Miranda stood, leaning over to give her a hug. "Just keep this between you and me, okay?"

"Of course, hon, and if you need to talk, I'm here."

Miranda gave her another squeeze and called the dogs, walking to the door.

"Thanks, Mom. I'll definitely let you know how it goes." And she would. Once she knew what she was going to do, herself.

COLIN CUT AN ORANGE IN half with one heavy swipe of the knife, then stuck a half at a time on the juicer, watching the pulpy orange liquid drain into the cup as he pressed the button. Lifting the glass up, he drank deeply. He'd been home for two days now. His parents were safely ensconced on a cruise ship heading to the Caribbean and he felt much better, though his memory hadn't even hinted at coming back.

He was returning to work today. Everything was more or less back to normal, except that he hadn't seen Miranda since she left his house the other night. He was still surprised at the turn in their relationship, and unsure how to handle it. He knew he missed her, though now he missed her differently than he ever had done before. Now he knew—mostly—what he was missing. He replayed that kiss they'd shared over and over again until his body was in an almost tortured state of arousal. He needed to see her, to touch her.

He grabbed a brown raincoat—April showers were in force today—and picked up his laptop from the mission-style hallway bench, eager to get the day started. Stepping out into the rain, he wondered if Miranda could be avoiding him. Had she changed her mind? He and Miranda were lovers—at least, they had been, for one, eventful evening—and he had treated her badly. He wanted to make things right.

And, if he was perfectly honest, that memory had been stolen from him and he wanted it back. He wanted to know what it was like to touch her in all the places he had only imagined, to push himself inside where she was hot and soft, to look into her eyes when they climaxed. He felt cheated. *How could he not remember?*

It was complicated, certainly, but there was only one thing he knew for certain: he wanted her and he didn't want to wait. If he never got his memory back, he was going to have to find a way to convince her to let him compensate for his careless behavior toward her and make new memories with him.

MIRANDA SAT IN FRONT OF her laptop, working on her summer appointment schedule in between clients, and read the e-mail from Colin as soon as it popped up.

Randi,
I need to see you. You're right, we should talk. Dinner tonight? Meet me outside my last class, and we'll go somewhere quiet. Let me know.
Colin

"What's up? You look a little tense." Penny sat over on the other side of the desk, sorting through some paperwork that was stacked there. The vet's office was closed one morning a week when the doctors did large-animal calls to local farms, so Penny was free. Usually she spent the time helping Miranda out with whatever needed to be done. It also gave them a chance to visit during the week.

"Just an e-mail from Colin."

"How is he?"

Miranda shrugged. "I guess he's okay. I haven't had a chance to talk to him since the other night. But he must be back to work, since he's e-mailing from his office."

"What's he want?"

"He wants me to stop by and see him for dinner."

"Sounds like maybe you were cut a break considering what happened with you two the other night, huh?"

Miranda usually told Penny everything, but she

hadn't yet mentioned the new developments between her and Colin.

"Yeah, well, in a way."

Miranda could feel the weight of Penny's attention and tried to ignore her by busily staring at her screen.

"Randi, I know that tone. What aren't you telling me? Fess up."

Miranda shifted uncomfortably in her seat. "Well, I had this idea…you know, the other night, when we drank all that wine—"

"Uh-oh, an alcohol-induced idea. That's never good."

"Yeah. I told Colin we made love the other night, you know, when we, well, didn't."

"You *what?* No!" Penny's eyes were wide with shock and she had to react quickly to catch the stack of mail she almost sent flying. She focused back on Miranda like a laser. "You told him that you two had sex?"

Miranda got up from her chair and paced nervously. "Well, we *almost* did, and I know he wanted to. He told me he has always wanted me. He just keeps letting my past with Derek get in his way. So I figured, you know, since he couldn't remember what happened, I would just give him a little…nudge."

Penny continued to stare and didn't say a word. Miranda dropped back into her chair, her face miserable.

"Okay, okay! I know. It was bad. Wrong. But when he left the other night, it was just so awful to lose him that way, and to know he won't give in to his feelings for me because of this stupid block he has. So, after his amnesia, at first, I figured I got a second chance, that he wouldn't remember at all. But then I thought, well, what if…"

"What if he thought your relationship had already changed? It would get him past his reservations?"

"Yes! Exactly! Then he could see that it really is right for us to be together."

"Except, of course, that it is all built on a lie. How do you think he'll react when he remembers that? Do you think you will have him in such a sex fog he won't care? This is Colin we are talking about. He's likely to freak when he remembers."

"Yeah, I guess. I know—I know you're right. I realized the other night that I needed to come clean with him before anything else happened, but I just… couldn't bring myself to do it. He *wanted* me, Penny. He told me so, and I just couldn't turn away from that."

Penny looked Miranda straight in the eye, sympathetic but clearly doubtful.

"So he wasn't shocked? He was happy when you told him that you two had done the deed?"

"He was, you know, a little surprised. But he didn't seem to hate the idea. We kissed."

"Voluntarily on his part?"

Miranda glared. "Yes, smart-ass. He was very willing, believe me. And later in the evening he followed me outside, and was, well…into it. He is definitely interested." She settled back in her chair. "But I know this could all explode in my face if he remembers. I guess I have to find the right time to tell him the truth. That's why I have been avoiding him for a few days.

He'll either remember on his own and be mad as hell, or I'll tell him as soon as I work up the courage."

Penny nodded. "Well, as long as you know you have to tell him, and if nothing happened except for a kiss, you should be okay. He might be mad at you, but you guys have been friends forever. He'll have to forgive you. Eventually."

Miranda stared at the e-mail again. "Yeah. I guess tonight is as good as any other time. No time like the present and all that."

"Good girl. I'll give you points for creativity, though. A pretty diabolical plan. And hey, you never know—maybe he'll reward your honesty with a nice, naked tumble."

Miranda rolled her eyes. "I wish. Probably more like a nice tumble out the door."

She replied to Colin's e-mail and made herself click the send button. There. Done. Now all she had to do was tell him the truth and face the consequences.

COLIN SMILED in undisguised pleasure when he looked up from the front of the lecture hall and motioned Miranda inside while he continued to address his class. A few students turned to take a look as she slipped into a seat at the back.

She watched him, feeling her resolve to tell him the truth fade a little. He was *so* handsome. By the way several of his female students were following his every move, she saw she was not the only one who thought so. She half expected the girls in the front row to have sexy messages written on their eyelids like they did in *Raiders of the Lost Ark.* And Colin was even hotter than Harrison Ford as far as she was concerned.

Most charming of all was that he probably had no idea. Slim and tall, he energetically paced back and forth at the front of the lecture hall, answering questions in an animated voice, then describing the next assignment the class had due. He obviously enjoyed his work. It was easy to see that he genuinely liked interacting with his students, and when he answered a question about no homework on weekends with a mildly sarcastic joke, the room rumbled with good-natured laughter.

Then his eyes met hers, and she felt the heat move into her cheeks when he aimed another slow smile her way. There was something in his expression that she had never seen before; his smile seemed full of naughty promise, and that sent ripples of desire over her entire body.

She was shaken out of the spell Colin seemed to cast on her every time she saw him when the students all noisily stood, grabbing their bags and jackets, and began filing out of the lecture hall. As they were leaving, she saw one woman in the front, a pale, dark-haired girl who continued to look back in her direction. The woman grabbed her books and walked up to the lectern where Colin was gathering together his papers and books. He smiled and took some papers from her. She didn't smile back, but seemed awkward and shy. Ah, Miranda thought, an admirer. Poor thing, she could barely look Colin in the eye and quickly left him, exiting out of a door at the side of a hall.

Colin strode up the aisle to Miranda, who felt more and more nervous the closer Colin got. He looked less tired and more like himself even with his bruises.

"Hey, Randi. Sorry we went a little late—lots of questions about the final papers."

"No problem. It was fun watching you in action."

He laughed as they walked from the lecture hall. "Oh, yeah, that must be why a quarter of the students are dozing off ten minutes into the lecture. I'm considering getting one of those super-soakers."

She laughed, imagining Colin turning the water gun on sleeping students.

"Well, all the sleepy ones must be male. The female students seem plenty interested from what I could tell."

They turned into his office, and he shut the door behind them.

"Huh?"

"Half your lecture hall has a crush on you, Professor Jacobs."

She chuckled as a ruddy color spread up his throat and he shook his head.

"Thanks for the compliment, but I think you're biased."

She grinned, absurdly pleased that such a small comment could seem so intimate between them. She definitely liked it. "Ah, believe me, we women know these things."

He crossed the small room and put his books on the desk, then turned to face her, leaning back against the edge.

"How about you? Do you have a crush on me, Miranda?"

She couldn't help giving him a little flirty smile, even though she knew she shouldn't. She was here to tell him the whole truth and nothing but the truth, after all.

"Maybe." Technically that *was* the truth.

His eyes darkened and the tone of his voice changed. "Come here."

She stood still for a moment, biting her lip, considering. This was not the Colin she knew, not the familiar friend she felt so comfortable with. He was a man, and a man with desire burning in his eyes. He wanted her. She thought about saying something; however, her voice was stuck in her throat. But her legs moved just fine and she found herself standing in front of him.

He reached out, slid two fingers along the strap of her purse.

"Have you been avoiding me?"

Her brow furrowed. "Avoiding you? I haven't been—I've just been busy since I saw you." Her excuse sounded less than authentic, she knew.

"Hmm."

His fingers drifted from the strap to her wrist, his warm touch sliding across the sensitive skin underneath, then down across her palm. Her fingers jerked a little in reflexive response.

"I had a lot to catch up on at work, and I knew you didn't feel well, and your parents were heading out on their trip, and I thought we could both use, you know, time to think about things, and…"

He closed his fingers around her wrist, tugging her forward. She stumbled and fell gently against him, their bodies now against each other. She tried to think clearly, but the hand that had been closed around her wrist had slipped around to the small of her back, kneading the muscles there, pressing her closer. His voice was husky as he leaned in, just a bit, and dragged his lips along her cheek, then to the edge of her mouth.

"I have been…thinking…about…things, too."

Each seductive word was punctuated with a nibble, and the next thing she knew his mouth was on hers, urging her to respond. A shudder ran the length of her body and her pent-up passion ached to be let loose.

As his hands drifted lower and gripped her buttocks, she groaned and placed her hands on his chest, her fingers curling into the soft material of his jacket. She opened her mouth eagerly beneath his, offering him anything he wanted and forgetting completely what she had come here to do in the first place. None of that mattered.

What mattered was that her body was on fire for a man she had wanted forever and who clearly wanted her just as much.

Her hands moved over the hard planes of his chest, feathering across his throat and neck. She stroked his ears and then sank her fingers into his thick, gleaming hair.

He stepped away and she made a sound of protest, but he squeezed her hand before going over to the door to lock it. Then he turned off the overhead light, leaving the office bathed in the glow of the single desk lamp. He closed the space between them, sweeping her up in a kiss that obliterated all thought.

She wound her arms around him tight, hanging on for dear life as he ravaged her mouth and ran his hands over her until she was desperate to get rid of her clothes and feel his touch on her skin. He was so hungry for her it made her own passion spike.

Then she heard voices, students passing by out in the hall, and it allowed her to grab on to one last shred of sanity. She tried to speak, her breathing labored.

"Col…this is your office…we shouldn't…."

He bit her neck lightly and then suckled the spot, sending waves of sensation traveling over her skin, and she sighed as he murmured against her.

"We shouldn't, and that makes it even better, doesn't it? I don't care where we are. I want to do the things I have been dreaming about. Right here, right now." He put his hand underneath her blouse. Resting his hand on her breast, he ran his thumb over her nipple in a repetitious stroking that made her whole body throb. He stared boldly into her eyes, daring her to reject him.

As if she could.

6

SHE DROPPED one hand between them and pressed her palm against the front of his soft, cotton slacks. Colin thought he might lose control right there and then, but it didn't matter; he wouldn't have asked her to move her hand away if his life depended on it.

He claimed her mouth again, reveling in the silken heat of her lips, her spicy, musky scent, the maddeningly rhythmic rubbing of her hand. He flipped their positions, pressing her against the edge of the desk, fully unbuttoning her blouse and pushing it aside.

He drew back and let himself drink in the vision before him. Her small, creamy breasts were straining against her peach-colored bra. Her skin was flushed, her mouth swollen from kisses, and her eyes were dark with need. She was perfect, as he always had known she would be. She caught him unaware, though, sliding the wisp of silk she wore as panties off, loosening them from one leg and then the other before lifting herself up to sit on the edge of the desk, regarding him with sheer, wanton lust.

"Colin, I want you. I need you. Now."

He'd imagined what it would be like to be with her over and over again—sometimes it was hot and fast, down and dirty, and sometimes it was slow and languorous. It looked like hot and fast was going to win out this time. He reached down, unzipping and releasing himself in one swift move. Remembering to protect her, he fumbled in his pocket for his wallet, but she pushed it from his hands, shimmying closer, her voice urgent.

"I'm on the pill. I don't want anything between us. Unless you know something we need to be careful about, I'm good."

It was all Colin needed to hear. "Me, too."

Then he was next to her, doing things that made his dreams pale. He nestled her warmth against him, probing and nudging, easing his cock inside her, groaning against the tender flesh of her neck when he was finally, totally enveloped in her slick heat. He stopped, holding himself within her for long moments, cherishing every second, every sensation coursing through his body. He was inside Miranda. They were locked together as closely as a man and woman could be. He knew this wasn't the first time, but it might as well be. He knew he would never forget it.

She moaned, raising her legs to wrap them tightly around his waist, her arms twined around his neck. She shifted and leveraged herself so that he could go, impossibly, deeper.

He watched her face as he thrust forward, harder this time. Her head fell back, intense pleasure in her expression, and he only wanted more. He wanted everything, all of her.

Bending over her, he withdrew slightly and leaned down to lave her pebble-hard nipples, then sucked hard. Her moans of pleasure filled the room, encouraging him. He loved how she dug her fingers into his hair, pulling his head tightly to her.

He pushed her farther up on the desk. Somewhere behind them he heard the shuffling sound of papers falling to the floor. Having found a better angle, he sucked and lapped at her breasts while moving inside her once again. She dropped back on her elbows to brace herself, panting with each hard thrust of his body into hers.

He was breathing hard, his muscles feeling like they'd turned to stone just before everything disintegrated, fiery pleasure rushing through him as he heard her cry out his name. She buckled, wrenching against him as she came. He braced one hand on the desk to hold himself up as his own climax drained him, almost causing his knees to give way.

After a moment, when he knew he was steady, he reached over and pulled her body up to his, holding her close for a long, tender moment. It was dark outside and he smiled against her hair, glad he had drawn the shade earlier in the day. That would have been quite a show for the students out on the quad. Rain still pattered against the glass, adding to the intimacy of the small room, and he rubbed his hands up and down her back, drawing out the moment.

"Miranda. That was…beautiful. I don't know what the other night was like, but for me this is really the first time, and I'll never forget it."

Miranda snuggled into his chest, feeling warm and satisfied, wanting to never leave this spot. She ignored the little twinge of guilt his words evoked. She felt too good to go there. Making love with Colin was the last thing she had expected to happen today—well, maybe not the *last* thing. But on some level, she hadn't really thought this would ever happen between them.

Now that it had, all she wanted was to have it happen again. And again. She wriggled against him, their skin sticky and warm, and he drew back, smiling at her as he pushed the hair from her face.

"If you keep moving against me like that we may not make it out of the office tonight."

She smiled back mischievously and was about to respond when there was a sharp rap on the door. Colin jumped at the noise, then put a finger to his lips.

"Shh. It's probably just a student. They'll move on in a second, but we have to be very quiet."

They waited there silently, not moving a muscle, though Colin made it difficult to be quiet as he massaged her breasts sensuously and trailed wet kisses up and down the column of her throat until she thought she was going to go very quietly insane. She bit her lip to stifle a moan and looked over his shoulder toward the door, hoping the person on the other side had left. It seemed he or she had. Thank God. She slid from the edge of the desk, reaching down to stroke Colin's half erection, determined to give as good as she was getting.

"I want us naked this time. Completely." His voice was ragged and deeply male. She felt a thrill rush through her at his demanding tone. Quiet Colin—who would have thought he would be such a take-control lover?

She was more than happy to accommodate, and started to lift his shirt up as he was pushing her blouse off her shoulders when the same sharp rapping echoed through the room again. They both jumped, glaring at the door.

"I'll have to see who that is. It doesn't sound like whoever it is, is planning on going away."

Miranda quirked an eyebrow as she observed the frustration on Colin's face, how his eyes had turned a glittering shade of gold. She felt desire coil between her legs; she loved this passionate side of his personality.

The knocking resumed and Colin groaned, tucking his shirt in, zipping up his pants and running a hand roughly over his hair. Miranda hurriedly buttoned her blouse and smoothed down her skirt, which thankfully wasn't too wrinkled, at least in the dim light.

She smoothed her hair and scooted over to the side of the desk to pick up papers that had fallen to the floor. Colin walked across the room, flipped on the overhead light and opened the door. Miranda saw the dark-haired girl from the lecture hall in the doorway.

"Nell! Is something wrong?"

Miranda could see why he asked. The woman

looked pale and tense. Miranda stood, carefully placing papers on Colin's desk as those angry eyes from the lecture hall moved away from Colin and fixed on her once more. Then she glanced back at Colin, looking upset.

"No...I...I was just worried. I came by to discuss something with you, but the door was locked and your light was on, and well.... I knew you had an accident, so I thought maybe you had passed out or something. I didn't know you had an...uh...appointment. Then I thought maybe you had left your light on, but I didn't have a key, so I just knocked again. Sorry to interrupt."

Miranda fussed with the papers on the desk, trying to be discreet. She was picking up a bad vibe from the conversation. Nell's brief apology was not very sincere. It was clear, at least to her, that Nell knew perfectly well that Miranda and Colin had not been discussing anything academic. Colin chuckled, however, apparently unconcerned, and invited the young woman into the office.

"I'm sorry to have worried you. I was just in here with a friend, we were um, pretty caught up in conversation and must not have heard you knock the first time."

Miranda rolled her eyes. Did he realize how unlikely that was? Sure, they were deep in conversation with the doors locked and the lights all but off. And what a conversation that had been! She put on what she hoped was a friendly expression.

"Nell, this is my good friend Miranda Carter. Randi,

this is Nell Maguire, my teaching assistant. Nell does a great job. I'd be lost without her."

Nell barely smiled at the compliment as she stared stonily at Miranda. Miranda looked at Colin, then at Nell, and stepped forward, her hand extended. Nell took it and weakly shook Miranda's hand, then turned back to Colin.

"I, um, wanted to discuss some questions students were e-mailing me about their final paper topics."

"Nell, I'll have to catch up with you later about that. Miranda and I were just on our way out to dinner, so maybe you can forward those questions to me by e-mail, or you can talk to me tomorrow?"

Miranda watched the woman's face tighten, disappointment clear in her eyes.

"But, they really need to know."

"They'll be fine. I know you want to help, but you have to resist helping them too much. The paper isn't due for four weeks, so there's plenty of time."

Colin grabbed his jacket and stood facing Nell, with Miranda at his side. He was polite but obviously eager to leave, to continue what had been interrupted, Miranda hoped. Nell was sullen; she had obviously been hoping to spend some time with her favorite professor.

"Um, sure. I'll e-mail you."

"Great—you know what, though? Take the night off, go do something relaxing. The e-mails can wait until tomorrow or the next day. The end of the semester is coming, and we'll all be crazy soon enough."

Nell murmured her agreement, tossing another resentful glare in Miranda's direction, then walked out of the room. Colin put his hand at the small of Miranda's back and ushered her forward, shutting off the lights, seemingly oblivious to any of the tension emanating from his assistant.

"Listen, why don't we still grab some dinner? It's not too late."

Now Miranda felt a flash of disappointment. She'd hoped he would suggest going directly back to her place. Or his. Her stomach rumbled. She smiled and took his hand, a small but intimate gesture that made her heart flip when he smiled back and squeezed her fingers.

"Sounds good. Where do you want to go?"

He lifted her hand to his lips and brushed them over her skin. "Anywhere, as long as it's with you."

"You look like total crap."

Travis sent Penny a withering look as he reached for his seat belt, then sat back, closed his eyes and dropped his head back against the headrest.

"Jeez, good to see you, too. Thanks for the ride."

"You really should give in and get a more reliable car."

"Reliable cars cost money."

Penny switched the windshield wipers on high and pulled out into traffic.

"You're a doctor and your parents are rich. What's the problem?"

"I'm a resident. And you know, doctors aren't necessarily wealthy, especially when they are starting out. And I haven't relied on my parents' money for a long time, you know that. Cars are expensive. There's insurance, you know. Never mind, I am too tired to have this conversation with you right now."

She frowned at the uncharacteristic edge in his voice. "So what has your shorts in a bunch?"

Travis sighed impatiently.

"Penny, I'm exhausted. I just finished a helluva shift and I don't want to talk, okay?"

Penny glared at him, though he couldn't see it because his eyes were still shut. She drove on, all the while bitching Travis out in her head. She knew he was working hard, and that he was tired, but good grief, did that mean you couldn't show a little common courtesy toward your friend? A friend who had gotten up, dressed and gone out into the rain to help you because your piece-of-crap car that you'd had since you were seventeen and refused to get rid of wouldn't start?

She stopped at a light, glanced over and saw that he'd dozed off. A lock of hair fell endearingly over Travis's forehead and she clenched the wheel a little more tightly, resisting the urge to push it back. That skinny, gangly redhead she had grown up with was handsome enough now to have any woman he wanted. Except for her. She ignored the dull little ache that always accompanied that thought.

Travis joked about the two of them getting together, and that's what it was, a joke. She'd only attended a two-year college. She worked as a veterinary assistant, and she didn't have aspirations to do anything else. She was a low-key girl. She liked pizza and beer. She read romance novels and liked horror movies, both of which Travis teased her about. His tastes were much more refined. And she was anything but refined.

Travis was a doctor—or almost a doctor—same difference. Travis wore suits and read thick novels that she had seen on his coffee table. She wore jeans and T-shirts and bought her stuff at outlet stores. He spoke two other languages fluently. She had taken two terms of Spanish and could only remember *sí, ola,* and *chili con quesa.* They were friends, but there were too many differences for them to be lovers.

She didn't like stuffy things, and while Travis couldn't be described as stuffy, his world was going to change when he became more established. He'd need someone who could handle fancy hospital affairs and parties, who could carry on conversations about art and current events, not someone who came home smelling like dogs and cats at the end of each day. If she was honest with herself, she felt good enough to be his friend, but far from good enough to be anything more, regardless of how much he flirted with her.

That's what made it all the more painful when he was kidding with her about them getting together. Or at least she'd always assumed he was kidding, until that kiss in the hospital. There was nothing funny about that.

She sighed and pulled back into traffic, looking for the turn that would take her to Travis's house. He had seemed so... sincere. Like he really wanted her. But he couldn't possibly be serious. Travis was hardly ever serious. He used to chase her around threatening to kiss her when they were kids all the time. Problem was, even if he was teasing, he'd been spot on about her wanting him. She had it bad.

Pulling up in front of his house, she shut off the ignition and looked over at Travis, who was still sleeping. His face was long and handsome, though more gaunt than usual. He really had been working hard. She knew that, like all residents, Travis put in at least seventy hours a week. Then there was all that studying he had to do at home. And she'd given him a pretty hard time. But that was just how they related to each other. Harassment was their main mode of communication.

She jumped out of her skin when he mumbled something and his arms flung forward in a panic toward the windshield, hitting his fingers on the dash, yelling someone's name—Paula? Who the heck was Paula? He was telling her to come back. Her heart pounding, she grabbed his arm, and shook him out of it.

"Hey, Trav, wake up—you're having a dream. C'mon. You're home."

His eyes flew open and her chest tightened at the sadness she saw in his sleepy, confused gaze.

He blinked a few times, trying to focus, and then seemed to remember where he was.

"Penny. Oh. I fell asleep."

She nodded. "You had some kind of wild dream. About someone named Paula. You were yelling and it scared the bejesus out of me. Who's Paula? New girl-friend?" Saying it out loud cut her to the quick, though she kept her voice casual.

He looked at her, his expression tense, then he rubbed his eyes and fell back in the seat again. "No. A patient."

"Why were you dreaming about one of your patients?"

He looked out the passenger's window and then back down at his hands. She was getting creeped out. This wasn't the Travis she knew.

"She, uh…she died tonight. A few hours ago. It was weird. I had this dream about her getting up off the examining table and walking out of the hospital—I knew I had to get her back, to make her stay, but she just kept walking. I couldn't make her stay."

"Oh, crap. Travis, I'm so sorry."

"She was seventeen. Heart attack." His voice was threaded with pain.

Penny sat back, stunned. "A heart attack at seventeen? Did she have a medical problem?"

Travis shrugged helplessly. "We don't know yet. They'll have to do an autopsy. She was an athlete. She collapsed during a practice, but by the time they got her to the hospital, I could tell it was too late, though we tried everything. But we just…lost her. Just like that. I had to tell her parents." He sighed heavily.

"It was the goddamned hardest thing I've ever done, Pen. I mean, I've lost patients, but never a kid, and never like this. Facing those parents, God….I *hate* this!" He struck out, hitting the dash, and Penny froze when she saw his rigid shoulders quake.

Travis was crying. She had only seen him cry one time before, when Derek had died, and then it was only for a minute, when he'd broken down during the funeral service. She'd been crying harder and he had been strong and comforted her then. Now it was her turn. He sat there, holding himself tensely by the rain-blurred window, in soul-racking pain.

Her heart broke for him, and she wanted to make him feel better, to let him know someone who cared was close. Reaching out, she laid a hand on his shoulder.

"Trav, there was nothing you could've done by the sound of it. Some things are just meant to be." She rubbed his back, urging him toward her, and laid her cheek against his head, shushing and saying what came to mind. "It's okay—it's supposed to hurt, Trav. It hurts because you are so good at what you do, because you care. It's okay to feel bad."

Long minutes went by, and finally he composed himself. He curled his arm around behind her and drew her down onto his shoulder. Burying his face in her hair, he inhaled deeply. Penny knew she should put some distance between them now that he was better, but his arms were strong around her and it felt so good. She didn't know what else to say, so she quietly let him hold her.

Her eyes widened as his hand started roaming down her back, and she shivered, telling herself to get out of his arms. The windows were opaque with condensation and she nuzzled his shoulder reflexively, her thoughts following her body's responses right into forbidden territory.

She made the fatal mistake of looking up into his face, and she was lost. His eyes, slightly swollen and raw with emotion, sent a sucker punch to her heart. His expression was plain with undisguised need for her—for comfort—clear even in the dark confines of the car.

Forgetting caution, she cupped a palm along his cheek, caressing the stubble that had appeared there at the end of his long day. She squashed down all the voices telling her this was stupid. Travis was her friend. He was in pain and he needed her. Whatever happened later, they would deal with it then.

As if he read the thoughts in her face, his gaze fell to her mouth, and she felt his heart drum hard under her other hand where she had it planted on his chest. The atmosphere in the car was thick with sexual tension. His lips were hovering above hers. When he spoke, his breath feathered against her skin.

"Penny, I..."

She slid her hand from his cheek around the back of his neck, closing the gap between them before either of them could give it a second thought.

"Just kiss me, Travis."

There was nothing tentative in the meeting of their mouths as passion exploded between them. Penny felt a jolt of desire as Travis's hands slid up inside her jacket, found their way under her shirt and ran smoothly across her back. She caught his lower lip in her teeth, tugged at it, and then let it go to return to his mouth, plunging deeper, exploring every corner of him that she could reach. Her hands ran over his sleek muscles.

She didn't think, didn't want to think. She simply let herself go completely. Her fingers slipped down the front of his pants, curled around his rock-hard erection and she began to stroke him. Extracting her hand, she lifted herself up and over, straddling him on the seat, pressing against him, moaning into his mouth as he tweaked her nipples through her bra.

"Penny…"

"Mmm? Oh, Trav, yeah, there…" She arched into him, arrows of pleasure ricocheting from the sensitized tips of her breasts to the core of her sex and back again.

"Penny."

"What?" She bit the question out, drawing back in frustration, their bodies glued together, their clothes pushed this way and that. She didn't want the haze to clear, didn't want a moment to think about what she was doing. Travis was breathing heavily, and he smiled in the half-light, looking straight into her eyes, right down to her soul. She sighed as his thumbs feathered the skin near her waist.

"You know, as much as I have fantasized about getting you in my back seat, your car is pretty small, and, um, my bed is only about thirty seconds in that direction." He tipped his head toward his house.

Penny leaned in for one more scorching kiss, then reached for the door handle.

"Let's make it fifteen seconds to the couch in the front room."

"Deal."

MIRANDA LEANED BACK in her chair, amazed at everything she had eaten. Good, lusty sex always gave her an appetite. Colin watched her from the other side of the table, humor lighting up his face as he sipped his own wine, and let her have the last slice of pizza.

The restaurant was not very busy. They had arrived well after rush hour and now sat in relative privacy with an open bottle of wine, an empty pizza platter and a huge antipasto between them. A small candle in a golden jar flickered on the table, next to the vase of fresh flowers. Colin gently slid the flowers a little farther away from the heat of the flame.

"You can eat like a marine, Miranda, and yet you never seem to gain a pound."

"Blessed metabolism."

"Must be. You're so slender I can just about span your waist with my hands."

The thought of his hands spanning her waist stopped her in her tracks and she smiled at him, remembering their encounter earlier in his office.

"Are you complaining? Would you like me to fatten up?"

He laughed. "You're perfect to me no matter what."

She tipped her wineglass toward him in salute. "A masterful answer."

"Yeah, well, in graduate school they had an entire course on how men could deal with the impossible questions."

"Really? Such as?"

"Am I too skinny? Do these pants make my butt look big? Is your ex-girlfriend prettier than me?"

Miranda broke out in a hearty laugh. "You know, men ask impossible questions, too."

"Like what?"

"Well…" Her eyes lit mischievously. "Okay, I can't come up with one right now, but just wait."

"Yeah, right. Guys don't ask neurotic questions, they just play golf and repress. Two time-honored methods of dealing with self-doubt. The worries don't come up because we bury them firmly underneath layers of machismo."

"I see. That must be why that show where the gay men remake the straight guy is so popular."

"How do you figure that?"

"Well, see, the gay men aren't so repressed, right? They have it out in the open. At the same time they are also men, so they know the things all men are worried about, but they can address them while the straight guy can stand around looking macho and clueless."

Colin stared at her, then burst out laughing.

"You think about this stuff way too much sometimes. But I suppose it's a theory. If any of my students can come up with anything that clever for a final paper, they'll get an A."

She grinned. "It's how I spend long nights alone, trying to unlock the mysteries of the male psyche."

He reached across the table and took her hand in his. "Seems like you've done a pretty good job unlocking mine."

She looked down at their linked fingers. "Oh, I don't know. We've known each other all our lives, but sometimes I still feel I don't really know you—you know, really know you."

"It's pretty much what you see is what you get. I don't have many mysteries."

She raised her eyebrows. "Really? Well, for one, I would never have pegged you as a lover who would take risks like the one you took back in your office."

His eyes flared with the memory of what had passed between them only hours earlier, and his fingers started doing evil things to her palm.

"What, did you think I would be a boring lover?"

"Ha! There it is—an impossible question!" They laughed, and then she became serious. "No, I have never, ever considered you boring. But you have always been so serious. I figured you would be more... conservative."

"Is that what you want?"

She stared him in the eye and spoke frankly. "I just want you." She twisted her mouth sideways, and glanced away for a moment.

"What's the matter?"

She shrugged. "I guess it should feel weird talking to you like that, right? I always wondered if it would, but then, when you were inside me, it was…perfect. It didn't feel strange at all."

"No, it didn't. I always thought it would, but it feels right. But when you say things like that it makes me…"

"What?"

He looked over at a family that had seated themselves a few chairs away and a sparkle lit his eyes. "It makes me want to do this." He leaned in and whispered in her ear, leaving her a bit breathless, the color in her cheeks slightly higher when he settled back in his own seat.

She pursed her lips, considering, and then spoke.

"You know, that idea would fit right in with this thing I read the other day, a how-to article on five steps couples can take to become more intimate."

"Where'd you read that?"

"A woman's magazine. But it had some creative ideas. What you just told me is something they recommended—trying something adventurous that neither has done before." She thought for a second, feeling the heat spread a little higher in her face. "I mean, um, assuming you haven't done that with—"

"I haven't. I haven't done that with anyone, and I'd like to try it with you. But I don't think we need a magazine article to guide us." He toyed with her fingers in suggestive ways that were sending erotic messages straight from her hands to her belly, making her more and more aroused as they sat together so innocently in this public place, talking about what they wanted to do to each other.

"True, you seem to be coming up with all the right

ideas on your own… Um, Colin?" Her voice caught, as he continued his seemingly innocent massage.

"Hmm?"

"I think we should go. I have to get home, let the dogs out…you could, um, come too, if you want."

He was already standing, leaving money on the table and grabbing his coat and her hand.

"Let's go."

7

COLIN GRINNED as he rummaged around Miranda's kitchen the next morning. She was still dead to the world—understandable, since they had hardly slept all night. Every time they'd looked at each other, or had accidentally touched, they'd spontaneously combusted.

Then he had awakened to the disturbing new sensation of a damp dog nose planted on his shoulder, and the sight of Chuck's large brown eyes begging for someone to feed him and let him out. After the dogs had been let out, he'd taken a shower and put on some clothes, then had checked in on Miranda, who had been still deep asleep. He should be equally exhausted, but he wasn't. He felt better than he had in years. Invigorated, even.

He still couldn't remember what had happened the night of his accident, but he cared about that less each passing day. He knew what he needed to know. That he had slept with Miranda, and then had been fool enough to walk out on her. Something she had forgiven him for, apparently, but he wasn't about to let himself off the hook so easily.

He poured a cup of coffee and considered their situation. He was almost thankful for his accident. Whatever had happened, it must have knocked something loose, ridding him of his prior worries. Now that he knew what it was like to be with a woman he had always wanted to be with—to really be with her, he wasn't going to ever lose Miranda again.

He grabbed a piece of notepaper from a little cube with daisies on it and jotted down a short note telling her he would call her for lunch. Then he stopped, the pen held in midair. How did he sign it? *Colin? Love, Colin? Last night was the most incredible night of my life, Colin?* He grimaced, going with his name and a few x's and o's. He thought it looked like a kindergarten valentine now, and he crumpled it up when he heard a shuffling in the doorway. Looking up, he saw Miranda, dressed only in a short robe, her hair a mess, her face sleepy, yawning like a sleepy cat and looking sexy as hell. His heart stopped. It was definitely *Love, Colin.*

"Hey, sleepyhead." Crossing the kitchen, he gathered her body against his and kissed her long and hard, while she wriggled and moaned in protest. He drew back, concerned.

"What's wrong?"

She brought the back of her hand up to her mouth and looked at him sheepishly. "Morning breath."

Grinning, he planted a kiss on the hand that covered her mouth.

"You taste just fine to me. I don't think we slept long enough to end up with morning breath." Stepping away, he crumpled up the note, tossing it into the garbage. "I was leaving you a note, but since you're up… I have to go and teach my morning class, but I'll be done by noon, so I'll call you."

She pouted prettily. "Do you have to go?"

His eyes raked over her as she draped herself seductively in the doorway, and he nearly reconsidered. But glancing at the clock, he knew it was too late to cancel, and he couldn't just not show up.

"Yeah, unfortunately. Nell could handle it, but it's not fair to leave her in the lurch, and I'm not tenured yet." He kissed her one more time before he headed for the front hall. "But I'll call you later. Do you have time for lunch?"

"I should. I have an appointment this morning, and then later today I have to meet with the shelter about my class schedule, but that's it."

"Great. I'll see you soon then, and I'll miss you until then."

With that, he was out the door and she was still standing there, exhausted, sore in all the right places, and wondering what in the heck she was going to do now. Padding to the refrigerator, she found the juice on the top shelf, and took out a box of Danishes, picking two. Hey, she'd had enough exercise last night that she could probably get away with eating the whole box.

She ate the Danishes quickly with a cup of coffee and went upstairs to shower. Colin had seemed so happy, so much freer than she remembered him being in recent memory. That was a good thing, right? Being with her made him happy.

Of course, the question remained. Was he happy enough to forgive her lie? It was really more of a fib, she thought. Ninety-nine percent of everything she had told him was true. It was just that one little detail she had tweaked. And he had left her that night, and he *had* hurt her. And, after all, he had seduced *her* last night, right? She wasn't sure how that was relevant, but she was sure it should count somehow.

She set the water to scalding and stepped under it, shocking herself awake and feeling the aches ease under the pulsing heat. Okay, so she was rationalizing. She would still tell him the truth if for no other reason than Penny would kill her if she didn't. She would do it as soon as the right moment arrived. She simply had to figure out how to say it to make him understand.

Toweling off, her mind went to the article, and Colin's suggestion at the restaurant last night. It was something she definitely wanted to do with him, but they hadn't had the chance last night. So maybe tonight. She would move them along to step two, experimentation. She made a note to stop by the store and pick up a few batteries.

COLIN WAS STUNNED.

He sat in the large leather chair in Malcolm's office, feeling completely blindsided. He knew he should say something, but he was unsure of what that was. His first instinct was to yell bloody murder, to proclaim his innocence, but he couldn't even do that!

How was he supposed to defend himself when he couldn't remember that night? He rubbed a hand across his eyes and looked at Malcolm, who had been very sympathetic and entirely professional about the entire matter. Colin raised his hands in a gesture of helplessness, then rose from the chair to pace the office. How could he possibly be accused of sexual harassment? What was Nell thinking?

"I don't know what to tell you, Dean Malcolm, except that this has to be a mistake, a misinterpretation of some sort."

"But you can't remember anything? You still have memory loss from the accident?"

Colin nodded, reeling from the news. He had thought it odd when he'd arrived at class and Nell hadn't been there. She never missed a class, but she was such a tireless worker that he had cut her a break. He would have preferred she let him know but, well, now he knew. She had reported him to the college for sexual harassment that very morning, and they had immediately reassigned her to another position until her complaint could be investigated.

"What did she say I did, exactly?"

The dean handed him a copy of the written complaint, stating that Nell had visited Colin's office on the Thursday evening of last week, the night of his accident. She claimed that while she'd engaged in professional conversation only, she felt he'd made inappropriate comments toward her, even suggesting that he wanted to have a more personal relationship with her, had touched her inappropriately and had even asked her out. Colin racked his brain, trying to remember, but he had absolutely no memory of seeing her at all.

He couldn't believe it was true, but what would motivate her to do such a thing? As open-minded as he tried to be, he couldn't believe he had actually come on to his teaching assistant. It had to be some kind of misunderstanding, but accusations of this sort could ruin his career.

Nell wasn't suing him directly. The college took the legal heat, according to policy. There had to be an investigation, and nothing was settled yet. But he wouldn't escape unscathed. It was a serious charge, and he couldn't tell his side of the story. He didn't even know what his side of the story was. He wished he could speak with her, but that was out of the question now. They were to have no interaction at all.

"She came to talk to me last night."

Malcolm was an older man who had been in the job for a long time, and didn't jump to conclusions, "Yes, she mentioned that," he said carefully. "She said she went to talk to you about the incident, to see if there was some kind of misunderstanding, but you had someone there, a woman. She felt uncomfortable and told you she was there for some other reason, then left."

Colin frowned. That might explain why she had looked so pale and worried. And she had said she wanted to discuss "something" with him. But sexual harassment?

"But if she thought I was acting inappropriately, why would she come to my office again, late at night? It doesn't add up." Colin clenched his teeth in frustration. "I don't know what happened last Thursday, Dean Malcolm, and I may never know. The doctor said the longer my memory is gone, the greater the chance it will never come back. But I know I wouldn't have done this—why would I? I have a woman in my life. A wonderful woman."

Malcolm shrugged. "I don't know, Colin. Men have affairs all the time. Being in a permanent relationship doesn't always mean much these days."

Colin's jaw clenched. "It means something to me."

"Take it easy, I'm telling you what others might say. I don't know how your memory loss will factor into this. We'll probably have to have some kind of statement from your doctor and we'll go from there. It could be seen as, well, convenient."

Colin felt as though he might burst a blood vessel. "You think I'm *faking?* Do these bruises look fake? Not to mention the fact that I could have died from hypothermia."

Malcolm waved a calming hand. "No, no, I know you better than that, but it's not up to me. There's a lot in your favor, Colin. You've been an exemplary teacher and researcher. You are ahead of schedule for tenure qualification. But this could hurt you, and I'm trying to think through all the angles. You're well respected here, and we'll get to the bottom of this, but these claims have to be taken seriously."

"Of course. What do I do now?"

"You go about your regular business, and teach your class. Don't talk to anyone, especially the media, and wait and see. The college has a duty to the student, Colin, but we also have a professional investment in you, and we stand behind our teachers until we have good reason not to. So, let's see what the lawyers and the board say, but I'll do what I can, pending the investigation."

Colin felt despair and disgust turn into an ugly knot in his stomach. His life was being turned upside down lately, for both good and bad. The last thing he needed was any more surprises.

IT WAS FIVE O'CLOCK BEFORE Miranda even took the time to notice the clock. The day had gotten away from her. She had one more appointment, looked out the window and saw Drew Moore pull up and park. Rap music blasted so loudly from the car that her windows shook. This was going to be a difficult meeting, and she wasn't looking forward to it.

Mr. Moore was one of her first customer referrals, a twentysomething with a lot of attitude. He was having a hard time with his three-month-old rottweiler, Diesel. Moore was angry because the puppy chewed, barked and basically acted like a puppy.

Miranda took the case with severe apprehension, because Mr. Moore was not a nice guy and he wasn't treating his dog well. However, she was willing to give him the benefit of the doubt that his behavior was committed in ignorance and impatience, and if she could help, life would be better for both of them. The first lesson hadn't been terrifically successful and this was the second try.

As she prepared for the session, it occurred to her that Colin had never called. Either that or she had missed him. But her cell showed no messages. She wasn't quite sure what to do. Should she call him or stop by his house? When they were friends, there wouldn't have been a question or a second thought, but now she had to wonder if she would appear clingy or desperate if she chased him down every time they missed a phone call.

Still, it was unlike him.

She put Colin out of her mind for the moment and focused on work. She watched Moore drag the cowering puppy out of the back seat and frowned. She was going to have to address this with him and soon. His behavior toward the dog was not acceptable.

They walked through the door, Moore first, as they had been instructed. Dogs were never to lead. The problem was that poor Diesel wasn't lagging behind out of respect for his owner's authority. He was just plain confused and frightened. Miranda could tell this by his body language.

As pack animals, dogs had a wide array of physical signals by which they communicated. Training a dog successfully was in part about knowing how to read those signals. Miranda's eyes narrowed as she watched Diesel shrink, a shrinking stance that essentially said, *I'm little, I'm no threat, see?* Though some submissive behavior was desirable, this was not. She felt her hackles rise but held her irritation in check for the moment.

"Good evening, Mr. Moore. How did you and Diesel do this week? Any particular problems?"

His face screwed into a snarl, and he yanked the dog's collar far too hard in the typical signal to sit. The dog did sit, and Miranda forced herself to speak evenly.

"Remember those collars are only a reminder for the dog that you are asking him to do something. A light tug will do."

"I think this one is terminally stupid. He doesn't do anything he's told, unless it's at full volume."

"You should never have to yell at your dog. Just use a firm voice. It's no fun for you to have to yell all the time and it will scare and confuse Diesel."

"He needs scaring. I don't know what this lovey mumbo jumbo is that you are teaching. I want a well-trained watch dog not an animal from some Disney cartoon. I came here and paid good money, but he's not learning anything."

Miranda took a steadying breath. *Patience.* She knew she couldn't expect every client to be a walk in the park.

"Okay, well, let's see how the walking exercise is going. Did you take him out for walks this week and practice? Two ten-minute sessions a day in addition to regular walks?"

"You know, lady, I actually work for a living. We did some practice around the house, but he just sits there and doesn't walk next to me. Sometimes I had to drag him along. I'm telling you, there's something wrong with this dog. Four hundred dollars down the drain. I wanted him for protection, but all he does is cower and shake."

Miranda clenched her fists, but kept her cool.

"Drew, you have to be patient. Diesel is learning a whole new set of behaviors."

"He doesn't learn *anything!* All he does is chew everything up and pee all over the place!"

Diesel, reacting immediately to Moore's raised voice, promptly peed all over the floor. Moore went ballistic and, before Miranda could interfere, he kicked the puppy soundly. She jumped forward, grabbing his arm, furious.

"That's it. You will *not* continue to treat this animal in that manner, Mr. Moore! You are to leave now, and Diesel will be staying with me. You clearly are abusing this animal, and I won't have it."

Moore dropped the leash and turned on her, grabbing her by the wrist and squeezing hard, towering over her. He was a very big guy. Miranda felt cold fear clenching in her stomach, but kept her voice steady and serious.

"Let go of me *now.*"

"You aren't telling me what to do with my own dog. You aren't telling me what to do, period. I can't believe you come highly recommended, all this namby-pamby, touchy-feely stuff—this entire thing is a rip-off." He squeezed harder and Miranda winced.

"I said, let go of me *now.*" She repeated herself as she struggled to remain calm. She could set Lucy on him, but she'd rather work it out herself if possible. Besides, she didn't want to take a chance on Lucy getting hurt.

"I don't think so." His stubbled face drew closer, and Miranda held her breath. "What do you say we work a little trade? You keep the stupid dog, and I get my money's worth another way. You may be a lousy dog trainer, but you're hot."

Miranda could smell the beer on his breath and for a second fear coursed through her and she couldn't think. As Moore tugged her closer, she reflexively bit off a command to Lucy, who was standing on intense alert in the corner. Then all hell broke loose.

A sadly yipping Diesel took off when one of them stepped on him, and Miranda found herself flung backward onto the desk as Moore was yanked away from her. Confused, she looked down to where Lucy stood growling, firmly attached to Moore's ankle. But something wasn't right—there were two sets of feet there.

She saw Colin, his face a study in cold rage, slamming Moore into the wall behind them. Moore slid to the ground, groaning, with Lucy still attached to his leg. He kicked at the dog with his other foot and Miranda commanded her back. Lucy was in attack mode, and she wouldn't let go no matter what Moore did to her. She was only part pit bull, but that part was all in her jaws.

"Lucy, let go! Come."

Lucy calmly dropped Moore's leg from her mouth and pranced to Miranda's side, tongue hanging out. Her watchful eyes were trained on Moore, who was cursing like crazy. Miranda reached down and scratched Lucy's ear to let her know she was okay.

Colin yanked Moore to his feet and looked back at Miranda.

"Call the police."

Moore lashed out, grabbing Colin by the jacket, but Colin was ready for him, knocking Moore back again with a hard, right-hand punch. Lucy growled once again, loudly. Moore rubbed his jaw and sent the little dog a nasty but cautious glance and scowled at Colin. Backing away toward the exit, he snarled at Miranda.

"I want my money back, or I am going to report you for setting your dog on me!"

Miranda raised an eyebrow. "Really? How about I bring charges for animal abuse, not to mention assaulting me? I think you would have a hard time convincing anyone you were a victim here. And I have a witness who saw you attack me. So I suggest you get lost and stay that way." She practically spat in his direction. "And I will be alerting local breeders and shelters not to sell another dog to you, you can be sure of it."

Moore hesitated, fury filling his face, but then he backed down. "Fine, he's worthless, anyway. I'll expect to see that refund check in the mail, or I'll be back. You can count on that."

This time Colin growled and walked up to Moore, pushing him back hard through the door, his eyes blazing. "I'd rethink that if I were you. Next time we won't call the dog off. And she'll stay attached to your leg—or some other part, perhaps—until the cops show up."

Moore stumbled back through the door, swearing profusely but looking less sure of himself, then he hopped into his car and tore out of the lot. In a flat second Miranda was on the floor with Diesel who had been cowering by the edge of the desk during the commotion. She murmured and petted, soothing him.

Colin caught his breath, his heart thundering in his chest after the confrontation. He'd been swamped all day between work and dealing with the issues stemming from the harassment case. It wasn't until late in the day that he'd realized he had forgotten to call Miranda for lunch as promised. He'd felt terrible, and hoped to catch her at work. He'd been relieved to see her office lights on and her car in the lot. When he'd walked through the door and seen that ape's hands on her, he'd felt more rage than he ever had in his life.

"Are you okay?"

Miranda looked up at him, her eyes somber, but she nodded. "Fine. Thank you. Better than this little guy is. Poor thing."

"Was he beaten? Is he okay?"

Miranda sighed deeply. "My guess is probably yes, considering what I saw here tonight. Though he seems okay physically. A little underweight, but no serious damage that I can see. I'll have one of the vets check him out tomorrow." She shook her head, looking down into the puppy's soft eyes.

"Moore only started lessons last week, and at that point I thought it was a bad relationship that could be fixed with training, but he is such a jerk. One of those people who think that training a dog means beating it into submission. Moron."

Colin watched the puppy, who was large and a little bony, quivering under Miranda's careful touch.

"What will you do with him?"

She shook her head. "I'll take him home for tonight. He's young and should be okay with some training in the right environment. These little guys are smart." She sighed. "I'll drop him by the shelter, and they'll probably place him with a rottie rescue. He'll be adoptable."

Lucy was still standing guard at Miranda's side and Chuck sat at his corner post, observing everything with lazy interest. Diesel peered out at them all warily.

"Um, you know, I was thinking of getting a dog. Could I have him?"

He was surprised to hear the words come out of his mouth. He really hadn't been thinking of getting a dog, but now that he had said it, he liked the idea. He would enjoy the company, and he didn't like the thought of that little guy having to be all alone in a shelter cage.

Miranda looked pleased. "Really? You would take him? A puppy is an awful lot of work, Colin, especially one that has been abused."

Colin sat down next to her on the floor, agreeing in a teasing voice. "I know if I keep him I have to feed him and walk him and brush his teeth every day." He grinned and reached over to scratch the pup's ears. "Well, maybe not brush his teeth. But if you can help me train him, I can take him to work with me and do whatever he needs. Dogs are all over campus as long as they are well behaved and on leashes. I won't have to leave him home alone that often."

Miranda's eyes shone up at him and Colin felt like a hero. "That would be fantastic! That is exactly what he needs, and that kind of socialization would be priceless!" She was so excited she nearly dumped the puppy out of her lap reaching over to kiss Colin soundly. Diesel decided to get up and walk around a little, checking things out. He was relaxing already, just being out of Moore's presence.

"Could I rename him? Or would that be confusing?"

"Moore probably never used his name in a positive way anyhow. Do you have a name in mind?"

Colin grinned, watching the pup as he padded around on his oversize paws, sniffing everything.

"Rufus. I always thought that would be a great dog name, but I never had a dog to attach it to."

Miranda laughed. "It fits him. We can go pick up some supplies. You'll need a crate and some other things to get through the night."

"A crate? But I don't want to cage him up. He's been treated badly enough."

"You'll see. He's a little older, so we may have to let him find his own way to it, but dogs are den animals. They feel safe in an enclosed space. We won't force it, but a crate is a necessary training tool. When you do have to leave him home, it can protect him as well as you."

"How so?"

"Well, from what Moore was saying, this little guy is a chewer. We can work on that, but in the meantime, you don't want him getting into things that could lodge in his throat, poison him or even electrocute him."

"Whoa. Okay. A crate it is."

As they headed to the cars, Miranda turned to Colin.

"Hey, in all the ruckus I forgot to ask how your day was? I thought I might have missed a call from you. I was hoping I would see you tonight." She turned into his path, bumped up against him and touched his face. "I'm sorry you had to deal with that jerk." She brought his hand to her lips. "But thanks for coming to my rescue. It could have been a lot worse if you hadn't shown up."

Colin leaned down and brushed his mouth over hers. "I think Lucy would have had it under control."

"No doubt she could do some serious damage, but he could have hurt her, too. I was so thankful to see you there." She squeezed his hand and they continued on to his car.

"So how was your day, anyway? What had you so busy you forgot about me?"

Though her tone was teasing, the day's events came crashing back on Colin as he loaded Rufus into the back seat of the car, which he apparently really didn't like. So, Colin let him out, opened the front door, and watched him jump into the front seat. This seemed to meet with Rufus's approval. Colin smiled at the pup, but his smile faded as reality reared its ugly head. For a few blessed minutes, he had actually not thought about what had happened at work. Miranda must have noticed something in his expression, because she was staring at him, worry plainly written on her face.

"Colin…?"

He sighed. "Let's get the dogs home, and I'll tell you all about it."

8

THE WORDS RANG outrageously in Miranda's head.

Sexual harassment? Colin?

He sat on the floor by the sofa, scratching Rufus's ears, his face tense as he related the events of the day.

"I can't imagine what could have led her to such a conclusion. It has to be some kind of misunderstanding."

Miranda jumped up, her voice a full octave higher than normal.

"Of course it is! There's no way you ever would do such a thing."

"Thanks. I spend a fair amount of time with Nell, and there was never so much as a hint of flirtation. She probably misunderstood something harmless that I said. I wish I could remember exactly what the hell it was that could have set her off."

"Do you think she's up to something?"

"Like what?"

"Well, I don't know, but anyone who knows you realizes you are utterly incapable of doing anything so…sleazy."

"Thanks." He disengaged himself from the sleeping puppy to join her by the window. He seemed calm, considering, but she was agitated on his behalf. He slid his palms along her shoulders and leaned over to kiss her neck, urging her to relax. "I love it that you have such faith in me."

She turned in his arms, sliding hers around him.

"Colin, I've known you forever. Even if we weren't lovers, I would stand by you. This is ridiculous."

He stared into her eyes but didn't say a word. She cocked her head inquiringly.

"What?"

He touched her face. She nearly melted with joy—it was a *lover's* touch. Gentle, caring, but not in the least platonic. As she had always imagined. And at last it was real. She turned her cheek into his palm, soaking up the pleasure of the moment. He rubbed his lips over her temple, murmuring against her soft skin.

"Sometimes I can't believe we're together. Really together. Ever since I woke up in the hospital, things have been surreal." His breath stirred the hair at her forehead. "You know, I used to dream about you. It was the only time I would allow myself to touch you, to kiss you. Then I would wake up, and it would all disappear." He stared into her eyes. "But now I touch you, and I know it's real."

Miranda's heart froze in her chest, and he sensed her reaction, pulling back a little.

"What's wrong?"

Tell him, tell him, tell him.

She smiled, effectively shutting off the voice in her head. *No, not now. Not yet.*

"Nothing. I just, um, was thinking."

"And here I was trying to erase all rational thoughts from your mind."

Laughing, she set her palms lightly on his chest, toying with the soft material of his shirt.

"You came close. Speaking of thoughts, um, let me see if I can take yours off your troubles. You know that idea you had last night? At the restaurant? What you said you would like to do?"

He remembered. She could tell by the flicker of heated interest in his eyes.

"I remember."

"Well, I thought we could try something, something new that neither of us has done with anyone else. Something that is just for us."

"And that would be?"

Her cheeks warmed thinking about it, and she felt a little shy suddenly. He prompted her again.

"Want to let me know what it is?"

"How about I show instead of tell?"

"Lead the way."

They made their way up the stairs to Colin's room, all three dogs following along behind. Miranda stopped at the head of the stairs and faced them.

"Lucy, Chuck, down. Stay."

Both dogs dropped in place on the carpeted landing, while Rufus looked on for a moment as if deciding what to do, then folded himself up in a neat curl near Lucy.

Following Colin into his room, she set her purse on the bench by the bed. Colin raised an eyebrow, unbuttoning his shirt.

"Need to keep an eye on that?"

"I, um, brought something with me."

She saw the curiosity glimmer in his eyes.

"A surprise?"

"Could be."

He finished undressing and she did, as well, and within moments they stood naked, drinking in the sight of each other. When they'd been together previously, they'd been half-clothed or in bed at night when it was dark, and Miranda realized she had never really *looked* at Colin. She had never seen him naked, not like this, completely open and exposed before her. Her man. And what a man he was.

He was gorgeous, but in a natural kind of way. He wasn't "cut" or rippling like a Calvin Klein model, but he was hard and strong. He'd lifted her as if she were nothing the last time they'd made love. The memory of it gave her shivers.

Her eyes drifted over his taut, nicely proportioned form. The summers he spent out on his boat left him with a tan that lasted through the winter, and his golden skin glowed in the low light of the bedroom. Her eyes moved lower, studying the sinewy muscles of his hips and legs, the proud maleness of his sex. He was already hard, jutting toward her eagerly, and she hadn't touched him with anything except her eyes.

Biting her lower lip in anticipation, she stepped forward, intending to change that. But when her hands reached out for him, he took a step back, his eyes hot, his smile wicked.

"Oh, no, not until I know what you brought in the bag."

Trepidation hit her like a quick splash of cold water. Would he be okay with her idea? What if he got turned off, or thought she was perverted? She didn't realize she was wringing her hands until he took them into his.

"You okay?"

"Yeah, I just didn't know if I should, you know, if we should…if it will be okay…."

He looked into her eyes, completely serious.

"I just want to be with you. If you have something you want to try, some fantasy you want to play out, I'm fine with that. But if you want to leave the bag closed, just c'mon over here, and I'm sure we'll do fine without whatever's in there." His hands closed over her breasts, stroking them lightly as he nudged his hardness against her thigh. "I think we have everything we need right here."

She shuddered under his touch, and smiled.

"Oh…that's nice… I, uh, didn't want to shock you or turn you off."

He brought her hands down and closed them around the velvety hardness of his shaft and she felt moisture pool between her thighs in response.

"Not possible. Looking at you turns me on. Thinking about you turns me on." His eyes glinted, and he sucked in a breath when she ran her thumb absently over the head of his cock. "So…bag or no bag?"

Walking over to the bag, she put her hand in, gazing at him furtively from behind her lashes. "You know when you said you would like to watch me, um, touch myself?"

He nodded slowly, his eyes never leaving hers.

"Well, when I do that, I usually use this." She withdrew a long, hard object—her vibrator from the bag.

She saw his eyes widen with interest. Or surprise? Her nervousness returned. "But we don't have to." She quickly shoved the vibrator back into the bag, but he was across the room in a flash, grabbing the purse, her hand inside it, his voice husky.

"Just tell me what you want to do." When pulled her hand out of the bag, her fingers were still clenched around the vibrator. His passionate gaze met hers. "Tell me what you want."

Miranda had never heard five sexier words. In a snap she went from feeling nervous to naughty.

"Well, you said you wanted to watch." She smiled secretively, walking slowly to the bed. Then she turned her head back over her shoulder to softly share the rest of her plan. "When you want to, you can join me. Or you can watch me take it all the way. It's up to you."

Colin's mind was spinning. Not only was he being served up a delicious male fantasy, but it was being provided to him by the woman of his dreams. The woman of his heart.

He walked to the end of the bed, resting his hand on one of the square posts of the sturdy mission frame. The blood pumping through his veins was heavy and hot as he watched her climb up onto his pillows, her pale flesh smooth and creamy against his navy-blue comforter.

She licked her lips and slowly twisted the bottom of the vibrator, and a low hum filled the room. Colin felt his breath catch, and he watched, his eyes hungrily feasting on every move she made.

"Do you know how many times I have used this, dreaming of you, Colin? How many nights I imagined it was you inside of me?" She slowly bent one knee up, dropping the other one to the side so that she was exposed to his hungry stare. His breath caught in his throat; he was mesmerized by her voice. She'd thought of him while pleasuring herself? He could die a happy man knowing that.

"Tell me more. What did you do?"

Miranda smiled, astonished at her own boldness, never letting her eyes leave his as she absently ran the vibrator over her belly, along her breasts, then down again. She had never felt this sexy in her entire life. She'd never even thought of doing such a thing for a man before, but with Colin, she wanted to break new ground, take chances. She wanted him to know how she had thought about him in her most private moments.

"I would think about your hands and your mouth…I've always loved your mouth…ohh…" She slid the vibrator lower, along the crevice of her hip, teasing herself as she watched Colin swipe his tongue over his lovely lower lip in a hungry gesture that made her quiver. The look on his face, the excitement in his eyes alone, was enough to encourage her to new heights.

"I wondered how your lips would feel on mine, how your hands would travel over my body, how hard you would feel pressed up against me, especially right... here...."

She laid the vibrator against the glistening folds of her labia and moaned, unable to speak as she pressed and stroked her pleasure points.

Colin's entire body went rigid as he watched her slide and manipulate the tool, her breathing becoming more rapid. She was close, but she hadn't let herself go over yet. He wanted to join her, but he also didn't want to stop watching. He wrapped his hand around his erection, squeezing and then stroking slowly. When her eyes opened again, she watched him touch himself, her brown eyes on fire with need.

"Colin, do you want to come here and join me?"

He could barely speak but managed to croak out something like "oh, yeah" and was on the bed beside her in less time than it took her to take her next breath. He covered her mouth in a desperate kiss, sucking breath from her as his hand traveled down, closing over the vibrator and taking it from her fingers. It felt strange in his palm, but he was fascinated nonetheless.

Stretching out beside her, his mouth delivered endless, deep kisses as he rubbed the shaft against her swollen, wet flesh. The plastic was warm and slippery, and he held it relentlessly against her, prodding her into an orgasm that had her writhing on the bed and moaning into his mouth.

Before she could catch her breath, he sat back, propping himself back up against the headboard.

"Come here, baby, sit on my lap."

Her eyes hazy with pleasure, she lifted herself up and straddled his lap, facing him. He lifted her and settled her over him inch by inch until he was inside her completely. He clenched his jaw, fighting for control. It felt too good. She wriggled against him, getting closer, deeper, and slipped her legs around back of his hips, driving him mad.

He still held on to the vibrator, laying it lengthwise at the base of her spine, rolling it over her muscles and massaging her back until she purred against him, moving just enough to create torturous amounts of pleasure for them both.

He moaned into her neck, biting the soft skin of her shoulder as he ran the vibrator along the supple muscles of her back. Then he brought it back between them, sliding it down to where their bodies were joined, and rejoiced in her hitched breath, his name on her lips, half moan, half whimper. She tried to speak, but her voice broke on another moan, though she tried again and got the words out the second time. "Let me."

He transferred the vibrator to her hands, sliding his around to grab her backside, kneading her against him. His head fell back when she carefully nudged the vibrator along where he was buried inside of her. When it touched his sac ever so slightly, the pleasure was so intense he cried out with it and bucked up under her, driving himself even deeper.

"Oh…Lord! Miranda…yes, sweetheart… again…."

The tight points of her breasts were scraping on his chest. Miranda became bolder with the vibrator, sliding it along his thighs and buttocks, down the crease of his hip and lower, seeking out every sensitive spot she could find. Colin was experiencing pleasure so exquisite he didn't ever want to come. He wanted to stay wrapped tightly in her hot, sweet body, with the vibrator creating sensations he had never even dreamed of. *Ecstasy* was a mild word.

Miranda watched him through the haze of her own, fascinated with his expressions. His face was contorted with pleasure, and she felt powerful like never before. She'd never been this turned-on in her life. He was buried so deeply inside she could barely move against him, the vibrator humming between them where they were tightly wedged together.

When he moaned her name urgently, she could feel him get impossibly hard, ready to explode. She left the vibrator somehow caught between them and framed his face with her hands, taking his mouth in a wanton, wet kiss.

As waves of orgasm overtook them, they kept rocking against each other even after the spasms passed. Locked together, their heads resting on each other's shoulders, they held on as their breathing quieted and their heart rates returned to normal.

They both became aware of the muffled humming sound that emanated from somewhere underneath them. Miranda raised her head, blinked and reached past her hip. She plucked the vibrator from underneath one of the pillows behind him. Picking it up, she twisted the bottom, shutting it off, and smiled at Colin.

"Boy, those new batteries really do last."

She shrieked with laughter as he playfully tumbled her over onto the mattress and pulled her close into his arms, tugging up the blanket.

"Let's see if mine can match it."

PENNY OPENED her eyes, not immediately recognizing the ceiling she was staring at. Then it hit her. Her eyes flew wide-open and she shot up in the bed. Oh, God! She looked to her left, saw she was alone, and then heard the shower running.

Travis. *She'd had sex with Travis.* Several times and in a multitude of creative ways. Oh, Lord. Her head dropped down into her hands. Blind panic set in when she heard the shower shut off. What was she going to do now? Looking around the room frantically, she saw her jeans on the floor…her underwear on the dresser… her sweatshirt—where the hell was her sweatshirt? She had to get out of here. She couldn't face him right now.

They'd made it up to the bedroom after all, but she thought she recalled losing the shirt somewhere on the stairs. Dashing out of bed far too quickly, she lunged forward into a headlong sprawl. Unable to catch herself as her feet tangled in the sheet, she hit the floor with a solid *thud*. Wincing, she swore profusely, rubbing the knee that had suffered the brunt of the impact and checking her shoulder where she had clipped the corner of the dresser. She would definitely have a bruise there. Great.

And that's how Travis found her when he returned to the bedroom from the shower, wrapped only in a towel, his lanky, luscious form still damp. Rusty hair curled tightly across his chest, and all she could do was stare upward, squinting through the tangle of hair that had fallen across her eyes. She swore again, helplessly trying to free her feet from the material wound around them. He grinned, crossing the room quickly to kneel by her side.

"Penny fall down?" He teased, but she noted the concern in his cycs whcn he found her lying there, tangled in blankets, rubbing her shoulder. She glared at him, glad for his humor and ability to be casual, considering their situation. If he had been all mushy and loverlike, it would have been much worse. She had no idea how to handle this.

He ran his hands over her arms and back, checking to make sure she was okay, but she felt the fires start along her skin even under his clinical touch.

"You're fine. I don't think they'll have to cut anything off this time."

"Good to know." She was relieved that her voice sounded normal in spite of the tumult of emotions raging through her.

His hands moved to her shoulders, massaging the sore one, then drawing her against him. He was warm and clean and nearly naked. He felt wonderful. She closed her eyes, rubbing her cheek against his chest, some of the panic subsiding. It was Travis. She smiled when she felt him kiss her hair, and felt her cheeks infuse with warmth. It was such a tender gesture, she melted inside. No one had ever kissed her hair like that before. It made her feel special.

"I need to get to my place and dress for work." Her voice was muffled against his skin.

"Call in sick. I'm a doctor. I'll write you a note."

Grinning, she pulled away, tempted to do just that but trying to remember all the reasons she shouldn't.

"Funny. I really have to go. Don't you have to get to work?"

"Not until three."

He stood and offered her a hand, which she took. She pulled the sheet up with her, wrapping it around. Travis looked amused.

"I have seen what's under there, you know."

She felt her cheeks get hotter, but she continued with their teasing routine and stuck her tongue out at him. She grabbed her panties from the dresser and pulled them on awkwardly, trying not to drop the sheet.

Travis grinned more widely, and she couldn't help but laugh, too. For a moment, she relaxed. Things were going to be okay. It was just Travis and Penny, goofing around, like always. They were just goofing around after about seven hours of energetic, acrobatic sex. She spoke, laughter still in her voice.

"I know. This is just…strange. I don't know how to act. What to say."

He let his towel drop, exposing himself completely.

She stopped laughing and swallowed hard. She couldn't help but look at him, and remember how he tasted, how he felt. He moved closer, tugging the sheet from her hand and letting it drop. To her dismay, her body jumped in reaction, her nipples hardening, followed by a warm tickle low in her belly. He looked her over thoroughly, from head to toe and back again, then drew her close, his lips just brushing her skin, caressing her as he spoke against her neck.

"How about, hey Travis, let's forget everything and everyone and go back to bed because I'm crazy in love with you and always have been?"

She stiffened in his arms, and he paused, then let her go with a heavy sigh, his voice light but strained. "I guess that didn't work, huh?"

Penny hoped he didn't notice her shaking hands. She got her bra and jeans on quickly, heading toward the hall to find her shirt.

"Trav, I'm sorry. I just can't deal with this now. I have to get to work. I don't know what... Last night, I wanted to be there for you...you felt so bad..."

His eyes hardened and pinned her in place. She had never seen that particular look on his face before and it stunned her. His entire, gorgeous form had gone rigid and still. "Are you saying what happened between us last night was a *pity fuck?*" he ground out in an angry growl.

She felt the blood drain from her face. "No! I'm sorry, I didn't mean it that way. Shoot, Travis, I can't think right now. We'll talk later, I promise."

He crossed the room, yanking her against him.

Anger—and hurt—blazed down at her, and she was unsure of what to expect. They were on untested ground now.

"We'll talk later. But you aren't going to duck and cover, then run away from me, Pen. No more running. I won't let you." With that he dipped down and covered her mouth with a steamy kiss that left her slack in his arms and shivering with the need for more. She trembled as his body pressed up against hers, hot and cold at the same time. She was unable to think.

She was in one hell of a mess.

9

COLIN SAT on the examination table later the next afternoon, patiently enduring the not-so-subtle chewing out Travis was handing him.

"I told you three days. It's been a week."

"Actually you said three to five. Besides, I'm fine. After a few days there was nothing—no dizziness, no aches and pains. Nothing."

Travis raised an eyebrow and slapped a blood-pressure cuff on Colin's arm, cinching it a little more tightly than he needed to.

"Well, it's not that I'm questioning your diagnosis, *Doctor,* but injuries and problems can surface days—even weeks—after the actual accident. There's a reason you needed to come back. It wasn't optional."

"I'm here, aren't I? Get your shorts out of the knot, bud."

Colin winced as Travis pumped up the blood-pressure cuff until his arm was pretty much numb, and didn't say a word in response until he took it off. Colin let the jokes go when Travis simply turned away, writing things down on his chart without saying a word. No catchy comeback? No sarcastic remark? Trav also had an uncharacteristic scowl on his face as he looked over the chart for a few more seconds. Colin pushed his sleeve down and inquired a little more seriously.

"Something wrong there?"

Travis looked up, and shook his head slightly.

"Nope, looks like you are more or less recovered. Except for the memory loss. Still nothing changed on that, right?"

Colin nodded. "No change. But I need to talk to you about that. You may, um…there are probably going to be some people who will want to talk to you about the accident. From the college. Lawyers."

"Lawyers? What's up?"

Colin slid off the table and paced the small examination room. "Well, it's bullshit, but they're going to need a medical statement from you about my accident, my condition that night and the amnesia." Every time he had to talk about this out loud, he hated it more and more. "My teaching assistant, Nell, has charged me with sexual harassment—"

"No way!" Travis leaned back against the counter, setting down the clipboard, his bad mood apparently falling by the wayside. His astounded expression was no less than what Colin expected.

"Yeah. She said I made some kind of inappropriate comments when she came to the office, and it happened that evening before I left school. Hours before the accident. And I can't even remember her coming to the office. It's a total blank. I'm supposed to sign some sort of release to allow you to talk to them. So they don't think I'm faking it."

"Holy shit! You have to be kidding me! They told you they thought you were faking? Are they crazy?"

Colin grimaced at Travis, who was increasingly outraged. "Yeah, well, that's how I feel. But I'm also blind with my hands tied behind my back. It's not even a case of her word against mine, because I don't have my side of the story. All I know is that I went to Miranda's that evening after I left the office, though I don't remember any of that, either."

"You were at Randi's? Does she have any more information about this?"

Colin broke eye contact with his friend, tucking in his shirt. "Uh, no. She has no idea."

"Why were you out in Old Port, then?"

Colin glared at Travis and tapped his forehead. "Um, amnesia? Remember? I don't know why I was there. Randi said we had an argument and I left her place. I must have gone down there walking."

"What was the fight about?"

Colin felt like a speck of bacteria under Travis's steady, curious gaze, and decided to come clean.

"Um, well…Miranda and I, we're…together now."

Travis looked at him cluelessly for several long seconds and then awareness dawned and his face lit up.

"Damn, buddy! That's great! It's about time!" Crossing the room, he popped Colin none too gently on the shoulder. "So she was as hot for you all this time as you've been for her?"

Colin smiled in the way that always seemed to happen whenever he thought about being with Miranda.

"Yeah, I guess. She said she seduced me that night when I came over. Though I can't remember any of that, either."

Travis fell back against the counter again, shaking his head in amazement.

"That is just too cool. I mean, it sucks that you can't remember—that's kind of a big thing to forget—but still. It's weird how things are working out, right after we talked about it—you and Randi, me and Pen—" Travis suddenly stopped speaking and the tension returned to his expression. It was too late, though. Colin caught the slip and pressed for more.

"You and Penny?"

Travis barked out a laugh that wasn't humorous at all.

"Yeah, but I'm not sure what, exactly. I had a bad night last night—lost a patient. She picked me up because my stupid car died again. I was exhausted, upset, and one thing led to another. We ended up back at my place." Travis looked down at his clipboard, but Colin didn't need to see him to know he was hurt. He could hear it in his friend's voice as he told him the rest of the story.

"I thought it meant something. Maybe she was finally willing to give us a chance. But she set me straight this morning. Almost killed herself in her rush to get out the door, and pretty much said she, well, you know, was caught up in the moment. She said it was because she felt *bad* for me."

He spit the words out between clenched teeth and Colin grimaced. There wasn't much worse than that. Damn. Pity sex was a pretty serious blow to the ego, even for someone whose ego seemed as bullet proof as Travis's.

"I can't believe Penny would sleep with you that easily. She's not like that. There has to be more going on."

Travis shrugged. "I don't know. But it's not the end of it, that's for sure. It wasn't just sex. I mean, the sex was hot, but you know, it's more than that. At least for me."

"You love her."

"Yeah, I think so. I want to find out. But damn, you can only get stomped on so many times."

"Yeah, well, hang in there. I think you might find there's more going on than you think."

Travis grimaced. "I hope so. Oh, and whatever I can do to help with the harassment charge, just give them my contact info. I can't believe anyone would seriously think you could do something like that."

"They have to take the complaint seriously. But the fallout remains to be seen. It's going to be hard to keep this quiet. Students are already wondering why Nell's not around. I don't know how my memory loss affects things, if it does."

Travis clamped a supportive hand over Colin's shoulder. "We'll get through it. And whatever I can do to help, let me know. Are you talking to a lawyer of your own? Sounds like it might be a good idea."

"I haven't yet, but maybe I should."

"I know a good one. I can give you her name if you want. I assume Miranda knows about all this?"

Colin nodded. "She's more upset than I am. She met Nell at my office one evening last week, and there was a little tension there, or at least Randi thought so."

Travis, who could always be counted on to find the sexual innuendo in a situation where there absolutely wasn't any, grinned. "Office nookie, huh, Colin? Way to go." Travis held his hand up for a high-five, but Colin rolled his eyes, ignoring him while fighting an answering grin. The office sex had been pretty amazing, a secret fantasy he'd always had. Even so, he wasn't sharing details, not even with Travis.

"Yeah, well, I guess it will work out. If it weren't for Nell and this amnesia thing, life would be really great."

"Believe me, I can relate. What's that they say? The path to true love never runs smooth? Seems like we're both going to hit some pretty deep ruts in the road before it's over."

"SO HAVE YOU TOLD HIM YET?"

Penny flipped through files and switched on the computer as she readied the office for the coming day. The doors weren't open yet, but Miranda had shown up early for a cup of coffee. Penny made the best coffee on the East Coast.

"Huh?"

Penny slanted a look from beneath her square-framed glasses. "Colin. Have you told Colin?"

Miranda grabbed one of the little wooden sticks that were jammed in a foam cup and stirred some cream into her coffee.

"Not yet."

She stopped stirring and made quite a task out of throwing her garbage in the can and wiping up the countertop. She could feel Penny's eyes trained on her the entire time.

"Oh, Miranda! You haven't told him yet? I thought you were going to do it yesterday?"

Miranda peeped over sheepishly. "I was—I absolutely was. But we both had some, you know, stuff happen, and I forgot."

Penny's arched eyebrow told her how lame that excuse was. "By 'stuff' do you mean hot, sweaty sex?"

Miranda couldn't quite suppress the smile that twitched at the corners of her mouth. "Well, there was that. But there were other things, more serious things that got me off track."

"Like what?"

Miranda relayed the tale of what had happened with Moore and then launched into Colin's sexual harassment charge. When she was done, Penny's eyes were wide and sparkling with anger, and it was fair to say she was no longer thinking about Miranda's omission.

"I can't believe that Colin is being subjected to this! Though it is so cool he took the dog! Moore is an idiot—I'm sure Dr. Rosenburg will see Rufus without an appointment. But that teaching assistant has some nerve! Poor Colin, he still can't remember! But we know he is completely innocent."

Miranda's head spun from trying to follow Penny's jumbled response, but she appreciated the sentiment even if she didn't gather all of the subtleties. Then a shadow crossed Penny's eyes, and her bottom lip stuck out in an uncharacteristic pout.

"Man, there must have been a full moon or something last night. Everything went crazy."

Miranda unlocked the doors and cocked her head.

"Did something happen with you?"

Miranda watched the color rise in Penny's cheeks, then drain again. Crossing to the counter, she leaned in close.

"C'mon. Spill."

Penny turned away and shuffled papers, glancing at the clock. "Listen, there isn't really time to get into it now. The first appointments will be here soon."

"Give me the *Reader's Digest* version."

Miranda was looking at Penny's back, and watched her friend's shoulders hunch and fall in a heavy sigh. Her head dropped forward, and Miranda heard her mumble something, but she couldn't quite make it out.

"What?"

Penny spun around. "I slept with Travis!" She clamped a hand over her mouth, having shouted her declaration out of frustration. She leaned back on the counter, looking miserable. "Oh man, Randi, what am I going to do?"

A car pulled into the lot. The first appointments were arriving.

"What went wrong? Was it horrible or something?"

Penny looked at Miranda as if she was losing her mind.

"Wrong? What went *wrong?* The entire thing was wrong. I mean, it was wonderful, in the sexual sense, but it wasn't good in all the other ways. I should never have done it, but there were some heavy-duty circumstances, and I gave in."

The car door slammed and Miranda cursed, wanting to pursue the conversation, but Penny's client would be in the door any second and besides, she had to get down the road to her own office.

"Damn, we can't discuss this now, but I want you to come over and fill me in as soon as you can. Promise."

Penny nodded and Miranda gave her a hug. "Don't worry, it'll be okay. We'll figure it out."

As she headed out to start her own workday, she tried to reassure herself with as much certainty as she had Penny. It would be a miracle if she was any better at solving Penny's romantic problems than she was at figuring out her own.

"So you already knew?"

"Yeah. Travis spilled the beans during my exam this morning."

Miranda furrowed her brow as she and Colin ran though the park, Chuck and Lucy behind Miranda, Rufus running by Colin's side on his new red leash. Warm and sunny, it was the perfect day for a run.

Miranda had missed running outside. She'd missed

running, period, and had only resumed it last month. Her leg ached a bit, but she seemed to have energy to spare today. Her physical therapist told her the mild aching was to be expected as she challenged her recovering muscles, but if she felt sharp pain, to stop. She figured they must be near the end of their second mile, and she felt good.

The Back Cove Trail was one of her favorite spots in Portland. One of the best parts of living here was that she could run along a different trail every day of the week, if she wanted. And there were plenty of beaches and islands nearby if she wanted to get out of the city for a while. She'd been to some beautiful places in her travels, but there was nothing like spring in Maine, usually made all the sweeter by suffering through the tough winters. She inhaled deeply, experiencing another sweet moment of gratitude for being alive, for being home, and for being with Colin. Did she ever imagine life could be this good?

The trails weren't very busy yet, though they would be as summer approached. Right now a gentle breeze drifted in off the water. The sun was starting to dip down below the bay, but they had plenty of time to complete the loop. Their feet slapped the pavement in an easy rhythm, and Miranda felt peaceful in spite of all the conflict in their lives at the moment. She continued their conversation.

"What did he have to say about it? Penny was less than thrilled."

"Yeah, that's what Travis said, too. She packed him

a wallop—told him she'd slept with him because she felt sorry for him."

Miranda stopped dead in her tracks.

"Ouch. Is that what he thinks?"

Colin stopped, walked back and began to stretch as the dogs scattered to sniff out the surrounding greenery. Miranda watched as he worked the powerful muscles of his torso, licking her lips a little when his T-shirt lifted as he bent with his arms up, exposing a sliver of flat stomach.

"Yeah, though I told him he must be missing something. I can't see Penny doing that."

Miranda didn't elaborate. It was almost the truth— Penny had come back to talk with Miranda during lunch, and she'd said she'd slept with Travis out of a need to comfort him, to be there for him. Though Miranda knew she wouldn't have felt those things in the first place if there wasn't something deeper going on.

However, Penny wasn't budging on the matter that nothing further was going to happen between her and Travis. She was very worried about how their one wild night would affect their friendship. Miranda cast a glance at Colin, considering how odd it was that for as long as they had been friends, she was hardly able to remember what it was like not being intimate with him even though they had only been lovers for a little over a week. It felt as if that was how they had always been. She liked the feeling, and a chill ran over her at the thought of it ending.

Colin walked over, catching her off guard, and bumped her backward playfully, catching her in his arms.

"How about me? Did you sleep with me last night because you felt sorry for me?"

Miranda laughed, sliding her palms over his chest, loving how the exercise caused the heat from his body to emanate in waves. Or, at least, she thought it was from the exercise. Then again…he had a look in his eyes that made her feel flirty.

"If I said yes, could we do it again? I could feel really, *really* sorry for you." She grinned evilly, and let her hands drift lower on his stomach.

"I think I deserve a little pity. I had that horrible accident, then there's the trouble at school, and now the whole sex problem."

"What sex problem?" Miranda leaned back, surprised.

He grinned, taking her hand and sliding it inside the front of his sweats. "I just don't feel like I am getting enough, you know, special attention."

He was hard as steel, and she wrapped her fingers around his hot erection, squeezing and stroking. She met his eyes directly, noting the small muscle in his cheek twitch and his hazel eyes deepen to a molten gold as she continued to stroke, standing closer to him so that she could reach more easily.

"Is this better? Poor, poor baby…." She purred against his lips, increasing her rhythm. A shudder rippled through him and she nipped at his neck, urging him on. He swelled in her hand and her own internal muscles clenched in response.

"Miranda, I don't think we…someone could come along."

She chuckled and ran her tongue teasingly over his lower lip, her voice husky. "Not if you come first."

Sucking his tongue deeply into her mouth, she pumped him harder, thankful he was wearing sweats so she could move somewhat freely. His fingers dug into her waist as he moved against her, giving himself over. Suddenly his lips tore away from hers, and his head dropped back as he growled a moan of pleasure. She caught the liquid heat of his climax in her hand, massaging him gently until he was left panting and holding her tightly against him.

She was turned-on as all get-out. He had been helpless in her hands, and she'd almost gotten off on that alone. She withdrew her hand, then captured his lips in a tender kiss.

"That was fun. But I don't think I feel sorry for you anymore."

Colin grinned down at her, vestiges of pleasure still warming his face. "You shock the hell out of me sometimes, Randi. But in a good way. In a *very* good way. It's like getting to know an entirely new side of you."

"There might be lots of sides to me you don't know."

He gazed at her through hooded eyes, lazy with spent passion. "I look forward to finding out."

Rufus groaned, having been obediently sitting at Colin's feet during the entire event, and was apparently sick and tired of it. He sulked at Chuck and Lucy, who had found ringside seats over in the shrubs, happy to wait. Colin stepped back and leaned down to scratch his pup's ears.

"What is it about dogs watching people have sex?"

"I don't know." Miranda laughed. "I guess they just wish they could play, too."

"Ha. Fat chance. I guess we can walk back to the cars. I think I've had all the aerobic exercise I need for today."

They walked back slowly, in the afterglow of their intimate moment, but it wasn't long before Miranda broke the silence. "Not to spoil the moment, but any new developments with the case today?" She watched his face tense. Moment officially spoiled. But she wanted to know. They couldn't simply ignore it.

"It's all on hold for now. They've reassigned Nell to tutoring for the remainder of the term, and I haven't heard another word about it, directly anyway."

"What do you mean?"

Colin was silent for a few minutes, and they walked slowly. When he spoke, she could hear the frustration and embarrassment in his voice.

"Well, officially no one has said anything, but word is out. I guess it was inevitable. I overheard some coeds talking on the quad today."

"What did they say?"

"Oh, just bits of conversation. One said she wouldn't mind being sexually harassed by me, and didn't know what Nell was complaining about. But one of the others was more serious. Said it made her feel creeped out." Colin shook his head, speaking through clenched teeth. "It made me sick—that they would even think it was true. I can't do my job if students don't trust or respect me."

Miranda linked her arm through his and squeezed. "Well, it's not true. And they *are* kids. They probably really didn't mean anything by it. How could they have heard, though?"

"Nothing stays secret for long. There are student workers in most offices. All that had to happen was for one person to overhear a conversation, see a memo, or for Nell to tell one friend, even in confidence. It doesn't take much to start a wildfire of gossip on a college campus. I'm hoping it gets straightened out before the college paper gets hold of it."

Miranda felt sick thinking about the level of stress he must be suffering, having to go to work every day, stand in front of that class, knowing they were talking about him behind his back. He continued, his voice tight.

"I don't know if it will go as far as the administration talking to students, but they are asking me to do an extra set of evaluations before the end of the term. No doubt the questions will be subtly geared to see if I have made any other female students feel *uncomfortable*."

"But that's so unfair! Students could give you a bad evaluation for so many reasons, like if you gave them a C or anything else! That hardly seems like a reliable source of information."

Miranda was clearly outraged on his behalf, and Colin looked over at her, appreciation in his eyes. He hooked his arm around her neck and pulled her closer.

"I love you, you know that?"

Miranda would have tripped and landed face first on the ground if he hadn't been holding on to her. The shock of hearing his words, the casual way they were delivered, with an affectionate squeeze of his arm, sent her into major palpitations. He loved her? Colin *loved* her?

They were back at the cars, and that phrase played over and over in her head. He didn't seem to think much about it, continuing on his way as if it was something he said to her all the time. They popped the dogs into the cars, and when she closed the door, Colin stood close, his eyes studying her face.

"I do, you know. Love you."

Miranda could hardly breathe, but somehow she managed to speak, even though her words came out on a wisp.

"I, um, how do you mean that exactly?"

He smiled and feathered kisses over her face.

"In every way I can mean it. I've always loved you, as a friend. I was attracted to you otherwise, but never let myself feel more than friendship, but I've loved you forever. Now I love you like a man loves a woman. And I love how you make love to me, stand by me, stick up for me. I can't believe you're mine."

Miranda swallowed and choked out one word.

"Wow."

Joy, fear, and other thoughts and feelings fired around in her head like a million electrical circuits gone crazy, and she couldn't sort out one single thought except for "wow." Colin loved her. Suddenly everything took on brand-new meaning. New depth. Including her lie.

She wanted to say something and tried to grasp the thought, but when he began nibbling at her ear she could hardly think at all, let alone speak. Then he whispered to her, passion and humor inflected in his tone.

"I'm hoping you feel the same way. I'm not just some naughty fling to you, am I? Not that I mind, but I was hoping for more."

She drew back and looked at him deeply, surprised to see a flicker of doubt in his eyes even though his tone had been light. What could she say? She had to tell him the truth.

"You are much more to me than that, Col. I love you, too. You're the only man I've ever really loved."

Joy leaped into his features and he squeezed her tight, but she felt the weight of her omissions more heavily than ever.

"Colin, we have to talk, though. There is something I have to tell you."

"You sound so serious."

She took a fortifying breath. "It's kind of a serious thing. But having just shared how we feel, I don't think we can go on any further without discussing it."

He narrowed his eyes curiously, and nodded.

"Okay. But let's head home first. We'll put the dogs in, get some dinner, and then we can talk, okay? Let's go back to your place. I have some clothes I can change into in the car."

She wanted to talk now, before she lost her nerve, but found herself agreeing. He turned toward his car, and she followed suit, feeling she was walking in a dream. This was either going to be the most happy or the most horrible night of her life. God, what was he going to think when she told him? And there was no doubt now that she had to tell him. After what they had shared, she had to clear the air. Things were getting too serious now.

She ran her palms along her arms, suppressing a chill, and slipped into the driver's seat of her car. The sun had set and the air was cool on her exposed skin, but she knew that wasn't what was making her shiver. Putting the car into Drive, she hoped for a miracle and that Colin would still love her after she told him the truth.

10

HER WORLD WAS a blur of steamy pleasure. Water streamed down her face and body, the heat penetrating her damp, cool skin as her fingers dug into Colin's powerful shoulders. Her knees were in real danger of collapsing beneath her, but she somehow managed to steady herself as another strong climax tore through her, causing her entire body to buckle against the slippery tile of the shower.

Colin moaned approvingly against her flesh, the vibration of the sound causing her to quake yet again beneath the ministrations of his mouth. He knelt before her, his face buried between her thighs, his tongue stroking and lapping at her sex until she thought she would pass out.

They had decided to hit the shower together—to be efficient, of course—and he was repaying her in kind for seducing him on the running path. She'd told herself she wasn't going to let anything else happen between them until she had spoken with him about the night of his accident. Then he'd asked her to join him in the shower with that hungry edge to his voice and the next thing she knew he was going down on her until she forgot her own name.

It was wonderful. She didn't care who she was or if she ever remembered her name again, as long as he never stopped doing what he was doing. Ah, there, he was using fingers now, too…*oh, sweet heaven.*

"Ahhhhhh!" The hollers went up simultaneously from both of them and they jumped apart as a cold shock of water sprayed over them. Fumbling to quickly shut off the faucet, they laughed and stumbled out of the tub.

"Damn!"

"I guess we emptied the hot-water tank."

They looked at each other for a moment, laughing. Colin reached for a thick towel, wrapping her and rubbing her dry.

"There. Warm?"

His face was tender, and she felt her heart melt. She loved him so much. How could she risk losing this? But he said he loved her, too, and what they had was real and strong. Hopefully it would survive her confession.

"Listen, why don't you get the dogs fed. I'll run down the street and grab something for dinner from the store. I'll be back in a few minutes." He was dry and already putting on his jeans—sans underwear—a fact that created a warm tickle low in her belly in spite of what they had just finished doing.

"Okay. And then we can talk?"

He kissed her on the nose. "You bet. I'll be back in about twenty."

And he was gone. She felt like an overcooked noodle from the exercise, the sex and the shower. Her head was a little light from all of that and the lack of food. Her stomach grumbled, thinking about it. Pulling on some comfy old jeans and a T-shirt, she also decided to skip the underwear, something she didn't usually do. The worn material felt so soft against her clean skin, the inseam of the jeans nudging her just so as she walked down the stairs to the kitchen. Heck, why hadn't she tried this before? Colin was definitely on to something.

After a short time she heard his footsteps on the porch. The sound of the key in the lock triggered fresh anxiety. Now was the time. In a few minutes she would sit down and come clean with him about her lie. Bracing herself, she washed her hands and turned to face him as he walked in the door, but the idea of their looming conversation fled from her mind when she saw his face. He was ashen, his sensuous lips drawn into a tight line.

"Colin? What's wrong?"

He didn't speak, but set the bag on the table and pulled out a local newspaper. Tossing it onto the table, he walked over to the counter, leaned heavily upon it and stared out the window into the darkness. "There's a story in the lower column...it continues on page three B."

Miranda was almost afraid to look down, but she did and her fears were confirmed. On the lower half of the page was a small headline about a local college instructor being charged with sexual harassment. She read the clip and continued on to the larger, half-page article. The report featured several quotes from students, most of them glowingly positive and outraged about the charge toward one of their favorite professors, but then there were some quotes that were ambiguous and potentially incriminating in their vagueness.

Two small photos of Colin and Nell were set in the upper right-hand corner, with a description of Colin's accident, the amnesia, as well as the action the college was taking. The campus women's-rights group chimed in with comments of concern for Nell and other female students, and the dean offered a neutral reassurance that the college took such matters seriously, but that it also stood by its teaching staff as one of the finest in the country.

Miranda was numb by the time she finished reading, unsure of what to say. Instead of saying anything, she walked to Colin and slid her arms around him from the back, hugging him tight, her cheek against his shoulder blade.

"How could this have happened? Can you sue them for some kind of invasion of privacy?"

He laughed, though there was no humor in it. "I don't think they care about the privacy of sexual harassers. They probably consider it a public service to let everyone know."

He broke away from her, his body as tense as a wire that was ready to break. Miranda took him by the shoulder and turned him to face her.

"That's ridiculous. This is getting blown so far out of proportion I can hardly believe it." She pushed his hair back, running her fingers through it gently. "I'm here, and so are all of your friends and family. No one believes you could have done this, Colin. The truth has to come out sooner or later."

He turned his face into her hand, nuzzling her palm. "Yeah, and if it's too much later, I'll be out of a job and unable to get one anywhere else."

Miranda didn't know how to answer that. The idea of his life falling apart like this, through no fault of his own, filled her with anger and helplessness.

"I don't know how this is going to work out, Col, but it will. There's no doubt in my mind that you are innocent."

He rubbed his hands over his face. "I wish I could get my memory back. If only I could remember what happened that night."

Miranda was painfully torn. She'd planned to tell him the truth about that night, but watching him suffer through this fresh trauma was too much. How could she add to that now? Tell him that she had deceived him when he was already at the breaking point? He needed his friends—and his lover—with him. He couldn't take one more blow.

Down deep, she wished he would remember, too. It would help clear his name and she would be free of this burden once and for all. She knew that was cowardly, but if he simply remembered maybe he wouldn't be as shocked as if she told him what had happened—or rather, what had not happened—between them the night of his accident. But now just wasn't the time. She looked at the newspaper still lying on the table.

"You'd think they could've warned you—asked for your comments."

He shook his head. "I don't think I should speak to anyone at this point without a lawyer, especially the press. Hell, I've never needed a lawyer. Travis said he knew someone I could talk to. I can't count on the school to stand behind me. They'll ultimately do what's necessary to cover their own asses. Parents won't want their kids in a class with a teacher who has this hanging over him. *Shit.*" He slammed his fist down on the counter, and she watched helplessly, searching for what she could do to help.

"If they fire you, we'll sue. We'll go to the papers, and we'll make a bigger fuss than they could ever imagine."

She was so angry she could taste it, and all she wanted was to get that woman, Nell, in a room alone for five minutes. She would make her come clean about what the hell was going on. Lost in imagining how she would intimidate the mousy teaching assistant into telling the truth and dropping the charges against Colin, Miranda was startled when he slid his arms around her and squeezed her tight.

"I love you, Randi." He nuzzled her cheek. "You're right. We'll fight this. I've worked too hard to let my career just go up in smoke without a fight. I'll call Travis now. I'll get the lawyer's number and phone first thing in the morning."

She squeezed him back. She would stand by him, no matter what, even if he didn't want her there when he found out the truth about that night.

PENNY WATCHED Travis's face darken with rage. She stared, fascinated by this side of him she had rarely seen—had never seen, really. Trav was always so easygoing and funny. But there was more steel in him than she would have imagined. He hung up the phone slowly. She gathered it had been Colin, and it looked as though the news wasn't good.

"Rotten bastards."

"Who?"

Travis shook his head in disgust. "Newspapers. They got a hold of the story. Pictures and everything. Colin's really twisting in the wind."

Penny jumped off the kitchen stool where she had been sitting, her expression as livid as his was.

"Let's go over there. He must be upset."

Travis shook his head, staring into her gorgeous green eyes. Man, he was a goner. Her hair framed her face in a wavy, wild fray, and her freckled cheeks were pink with outrage. He remembered how her creamy skin had felt against his and he swallowed, his body responding immediately to the memory.

"No, he's at Miranda's. We'd best just leave them to deal with it and talk to them tomorrow. I gave him the number of a lawyer friend."

"It's that bad? He needs a lawyer?"

Travis grimaced. "Sounds like it."

"Well, good thing that Randi is there. She'll calm him down, take his mind off things."

Travis walked to the fridge and took out a beer, grabbing one for Penny, too. Reaching to the back of the shelf, he took his time, feeling a little guilty. They could have gone to Miranda's, but he wanted this time alone with Penny. They had to talk.

He'd stopped by her apartment on a whim, not sure how she would respond to him after their argument that morning. He knew he'd been a little overbearing— well, maybe a lot—but he had been so pissed off. So hurt.

It was late evening, but when she found him at the door, she had acted as if nothing had happened between them. She was seemingly without a care in the world. He didn't know if he should be relieved or pissed off again. The previous night's passionate encounter might never have happened. It was irking the hell out of him, but he was playing it her way for the moment.

"It's cool that they're together." Penny popped the cap off her beer and took a swig.

When she set it back on the counter and swiped her lips with her tongue to catch some stray drops, Travis almost had to bite back a groan. That tiny mouth had done some incredible things to him.

"I just hope it holds together," she added.

"Why wouldn't it? They've been crazy about each other forever, just took their time realizing it." *Kind of like us,* he added silently.

Penny's expression turned pensive.

"Well, it's not quite as simple as that."

"How so?"

"Miranda—well, shoot—if I tell you this you *can't* tell anyone else. Especially Colin. That's up to Miranda."

Travis's curiosity was piqued and he slid up onto the stool next to hers, letting his knee brush her thigh. Her reaction told him she wasn't as immune to him as she appeared, thank God.

"Okay. I can keep a secret."

"Good, because I'm breaking one to tell you."

He gazed into her eyes, wanting to connect. "You trust me?"

She looked at him for another second and then nodded, her voice low. "I trust you, Trav. You know that."

"Okay. So fess up."

Penny related the story of Miranda's plan to seduce Colin, and though she did so, she stopped short of sharing her opinion on the subject, thrown off by Travis's wide, approving grin.

"You think this is funny?"

"Funny? I think it's great! Good for her! One of them finally had to get the nerve to step in and do something. Something had to shake Colin up a little. I love the guy, but he can be too much of a Boy Scout sometimes."

He could tell from Penny's face that she couldn't disagree more.

"She lied to him, Travis—a *big* lie—to get him to sleep with her. That's not exactly a good foundation to build a relationship on. She took advantage of him when he was hurt. I would be royally pissed if I were in his shoes."

Travis looked at her, adoring the snap of indignation, the honesty that was part and parcel of Penny. Feeling the world shrink down to just the two of them, he cupped her cheek in his hand, stroking her soft skin. She didn't draw away, and he could see the pulse at the base of her throat throb.

"Penny, she loves him. She's going for it all. She may have made a risky move, but it's better than never trying at all. Sometimes you have to lay it all on the line when you love someone. You can't just play it safe forever."

She left her seat, disengaging herself from his touch. He let her go, for the moment. Watching her wrap her arms across her front, he wondered if she knew how much she was telling him without saying a word, how vulnerable and confused she looked. Hope surged within him. She wouldn't be here with him now, she wouldn't let him touch her like that if she didn't feel more than friendship or pity for him.

"Well, she's risking everything, that's for sure. She might lose it all, including his friendship."

"Maybe she thinks it's worth the risk. Maybe that loss would be better than going on loving someone and never taking the chance."

She met his eyes then, seemingly torn with indecision and desire, and he took his own risk. Crossing the room, he took her in his arms. She was tense, but her small body fit next to his perfectly, her curves pressing softly up against his straight lines. He had to make her see.

"Do you think I'm worth the risk, Pen?"

"I…I don't want to lose what we have."

"And what's that, exactly?"

"You're my friend, Travis. I won't lie to you. You know I want you, but I don't want to put our friendship on the line for sex."

He stared down into her beautiful, confused face for a moment and took in the soft flowery scent of her hair.

"You think that's **all** this is? Just sex? What if it's more? What if I'm willing to risk it, Penny? I don't think I want to be just your friend anymore."

She became still in his arms.

"What do you mean? Trav, we've been friends forever. You don't just throw away something like that."

Before she could say another word, he kissed her. Long, slow and sweet, until they were both quivering. When he drew away and set his forehead against hers, they were both breathing heavily. He knew his voice was unsteady but he didn't care. He would open himself to her even if he risked having her rip his heart out in the process.

"Do you feel that, Penny? What's between us? I've never been affected by anyone like I am by you, and that's not something we should throw away, either."

"Travis, shoot, I don't know what to do."

"How about me?" He laughed, but there was an underlying seriousness in his tone and in the way he touched her.

"No…yes…I can't think when you do that…."

He did it some more, letting his hands travel up and down her arms, softly grazing the outside of her breasts on each pass.

"Good. Don't think. Not thinking is good."

She laughed, pushing at his chest, but not so hard as to actually separate herself. "Cut it out—this isn't funny."

He stared down into her face, glad to see the tension fading though her confusion remained.

"No, it's not funny. I don't know what the problem is, Pen." He lifted her fingers to his mouth, kissing each one in turn, his eyes never leaving hers. "I know you want me, so what's the problem?"

Her breath hitched, and he nuzzled her gently.

"I do want you."

"Then there's no problem, right?"

"It's just that…you know…"

"What?"

Penny looked up into Travis's face. He was a man who wanted her, but she was still looking into the face of her friend. She owed him the truth.

"I just…God, this is so lame, I know. I want this as much now as you do, but later on, when it ends, I don't know how it will affect us."

"I think I've made it clear we can never only be friends again, Penny. I want more than that."

She frowned. "Well, it's not like we can get married or anything."

He blinked, obviously taken by surprise. "Well, not this weekend, but who knows? Maybe eventually."

"No, I mean ever."

Now the teasing light was gone altogether. "And exactly why not?"

She looked away, nervous, but he tilted her chin toward him, forcing her gaze to meet his.

"Why not?"

"You need...I mean, I figured you would want, um, a...shoot, Travis—you know, you are a *doctor!*"

Lips pursed, he nodded. "Well, yes I am. I don't see the connection. Most women want to marry a handsome doctor, and yet this seems to be a strike against me with you?"

She blew out a frustrated sigh. "I am a vet's assistant, Trav. I went to two-year college. I don't wear dresses that often, read big books or dance—well, not the slow-dancing. I didn't grow up the same way you did. I don't even have a father to give me away if I ever get married."

He shook his head, looking more confused. "Penny, I have no idea what the hell you're getting at. How does any of that mean you can't be with me?"

"God, you're so thick sometimes!" She looked up at him, her eyes blazing with frustration. "You'll be a doctor soon. You will need someone who's your equal, just as smart, able to dress up and plan parties and do all that—" she waved her hands around, tears stinging the back of her eyes "—all the stuff that a doctor's wife has to do. I'm no high-society girl. And I don't want to be."

Travis stared, clearly shocked. She bit her lip, forcing back the stupid tears that had threatened, and crossed her arms tightly in front of her. She looked down, feeling a bit childish, but at least she had finally said it. She didn't know what to expect, but the last thing she would have guessed was to hear him laughing.

"What's so funny?"

He smiled more widely.

"Penny, you are such a nut."

She had no idea how to respond. What was he up to?

He drew her close to him. She felt his chest rise and fall against her, and she rested her face on his shoulder. Then he started to hum, and sway back and forth. She wrinkled her brow, wondering what he was doing, vaguely recognizing the song he was humming. He was slightly off-key, so she had to listen a little more closely.

She smiled when she recognized it. "Crazy for You." His hand slid down and his fingers meshed with hers. She started to pull away, but his other arm trapped her close to him. She stiffened and fumbled, and when she started to object again, he lowered his mouth to hers, humming against her lips, melting her objections away. She relaxed against him, as they danced around the room.

He stopped humming and the kiss became deeper and hotter, until she was shaking with need for him, and he mumbled against her mouth. "You dance just fine."

"Travis, I don't—"

He put a finger to her lips.

"Pen, whatever idea you have in your head about not being good enough for me is just stupid. And you are not a stupid woman. In fact, you are probably too good for me. This is what I'm going to do about it. I'm going to make love to you, and I'm going to keep making love to you until you have no choice but to fall so completely head over heels for me that you get over all this non-sense." He grinned, lowering his mouth closer to hers. "Resistance is futile, woman, so I suggest you get used to the idea."

Desire swamped her as she struggled to remember why she shouldn't be doing this, but with his hands hot on her skin, she couldn't remember. In so far as making her fall in love with him, he wouldn't have to work very hard—or at all.

COLIN STRETCHED out on the couch, flipping channels, trying to blank out any thoughts about meetings with lawyers and the newspaper article. He didn't want to think. There was nothing he could do at the moment anyway. Miranda was in front of her laptop, research-ing new training techniques. She was worlds away from him. He felt bored and restless, but didn't want to dis-tract her from her work.

He picked up a somewhat beat-up magazine from the table. Great. A women's magazine. Well, what the heck. He had never looked at one of these. Maybe he would find the secrets to unlocking the mysteries of the female psyche. In fact, now that he thought about it he became more curious.

He had seen the rows upon rows of romance and relationship novels at the bookstore—women wrote a *lot*. But how often did men read those tomes? He'd seen his female students looking through *Maxim,* and knew they read Stephen King, John Grisham, and the like, but he could honestly say he had never seen a male student reading *Cosmopolitan* or reading, well, whoever the great romance authors were. He'd seen Penny's romance novels in her apartment but hadn't really paid attention. Why not?

His mind started ticking away with research ideas. How did male and female reading habits affect the sexes? Did they reinforce certain stereotypes? He suspected men were on the losing end. Women read men's literature, but not vice versa. Men could very well be missing out on a mother lode of information on the fair sex. From the horse's mouth, as it were.

Intrigued, he stared at the cover, reading the headlines—well, okay, maybe not—but he would find out how to jump-start his love life in five easy steps. He grinned and started flipping through the glossy pages.

Locating the cover story, the realization hit him that this must be the article Miranda had talked about, the one that had ideas for how to become more intimate. Intrigued, he read further. Women's magazines were apparently pretty sexually explicit—not exactly what he had expected. There were mind-bogglingly detailed descriptions of anatomy and "things to do," sexual techniques and positions, etc. Thinking about Miranda reading this was a bit of a turn-on. He wriggled on the soft cushion of the sofa, readjusting a little. No, scratch that—it was definitely a total turn-on.

He read through the suggestions and found them smart and realistic, assuming both partners were cooperative. The first was to take control—insightfully suggesting women risk rejection as men had done for centuries. He supposed she had done that when she seduced him in the first place. He hadn't rejected her, but he had walked out, a fact he was still trying to make peace with.

The second was—whoa—to try something neither partner had done before. His mind drifted to memories of the vibrator, and Miranda's question about if he had shared anything like that with someone else. He was stiff as a board now, and shifted again, trying to keep his attention on the article.

Well, let's look at number three, he thought, turning the page. *Explore: Go away. Go somewhere new.* That was good advice. For many couples a change of pace and location could inspire and refresh passionate feelings. Place was tightly tied to how the mind worked. Just like old, familiar places bring comfort and make us feel secure, a new place could make lovers feel daring and revitalized.

He looked at Miranda, who was still gazing into the computer screen, mumbling occasionally. She was so amazingly beautiful it took his breath away. She didn't feel so much like the friend he had grown up with now as his lover—*his woman.*

A smile quirked at the edge of his mouth, prompted

by the discovery that he was capable of such masculine possessiveness. So much for being an enlightened male of the twenty-first century. Miranda stoked every buried caveman instinct. Why she thought she needed any kind of hints and tips to seduce him was unfathomable, but still, he couldn't complain about the results.

"Hey."

She didn't even blink, completely into whatever had her attention on the screen. Closing the magazine, he scooted over on the sofa and pushed the curtain of silky hair back, planting a wet kiss on the shell of her ear, sliding his tongue inside and flicking gently. It was a move he had discovered drove her wild when they were making love, and it didn't disappoint now. She arched her head back, a husky chuckle rising from her throat. When he dragged his lips down the line of her jaw, he gloried in the sharp breath she took. He looked down with satisfaction to see her nipples pebbled against her sweatshirt.

"You were completely ignoring me. I had to resort to drastic measures to get you away from that computer."

She smiled, and slid the laptop onto the table.

"I'm sorry, Colin. I do get lost while reading the search-and-rescue material. I am dying to be able to do that. I could adopt more dogs, train them, find places for them to work, give them purpose and help people in trouble…like the ones who were with the team that found me when I had my accident."

"They had search animals?"

"Yeah. They tracked my cell-phone signal, but the dogs actually reached me first. Their barking led the team to my exact spot."

"Jesus, Randi, when I think of you out there alone, it kills me."

She kissed him softly. "It was a stupid move on my part, going up there alone. I should've known better, and I was lucky. More than lucky. In some ways I am very grateful. It brought me back home, to you. And to my new business. I have to be grateful for all of that."

Colin nodded, listening to her, but also distracted by the pink flush in her cheeks that he knew his kisses had caused.

"Listen, I was thinking..."

"Hmm?"

"What do you think about getting away for a while?"

"What'd you have in mind?"

"Something quick, a weekend, maybe—away from all the craziness and newspapers—just somewhere we could be alone."

He could tell by the warmth in her eyes that she liked the idea a lot. His glance drifted to the magazine on the table, and he saw a flicker of a question in her eyes, but then it was overcome by her smile.

"That would be nice. Good timing, too. I actually have this weekend free. No appointments."

He nodded. "I can be out early tomorrow. In fact, I will make sure I am. Hanging around campus is the last thing I want to do, and I can talk with the lawyer on

Monday. I doubt she would be able to see me tomorrow anyway."

"So where did you want to go?"

"Well, we can't go too far away, I suppose. But it's not the busy season yet, so why don't I look for some inns, maybe head north? We'll take off tomorrow afternoon."

She smiled, then ran her fingers over his hair, and his body went into overdrive from the simple caress.

"Maybe we should just drive—we'll go, and stop where we find a place to stay."

"Feeling adventurous?"

Her cheeks warmed and the look she shared with him didn't even pretend to mask what she was thinking. "Most definitely."

For one blissful moment Colin felt his cares fall away, replaced by a heady sense of anticipation.

"Then that's what we'll do, tomorrow. I'll pick you up after my class, around ten. For the moment, I have some other ideas." His hand slipped over the gentle slope of her breast, and squeezed. She turned her head, bringing her face closer to his, excitement building between them.

"Like what?"

He moved in closer, his touch more insistent, his mouth only a breath away from hers. "Let me show you."

11

Miranda held the thin baby-doll in front of her, wondering if she should even pack it. A wicked smile claimed her lips. They didn't usually bother with any kind of pajamas, but she had never really dressed up sexy for Colin, well, except for the time he didn't remember, so maybe it would be a treat. Grabbing some jeans and sweaters, she zipped up her bag and hauled it into the front room.

While packing, she'd decided that telling Colin about the night of their accident had become all but impossible. She'd tried, she really had, but something was always getting in the way. For now, she was putting it out of her mind. She loved him, and she wanted to enjoy what they were sharing. The future and the past would have to take care of themselves. The phone rang, and she picked it up and answered without hesitation.

"Hey, Pen."

"How'd you know it was me?"

Miranda shrugged, nearly letting the phone slide from her shoulder as she grabbed for a coat from the rack.

"I have spies everywhere." Miranda grinned into the

phone. "Seriously, I just assumed you were returning my call."

"Yeah, sorry I had to cut you short this morning, all hell was breaking loose here. Mrs. Paul brought her cats in, and of course one of them wiggled loose, and the Meyers's dog went nuts. They were all over the place."

Miranda laughed. She'd been present once when Mrs. Paul came in with her cats and it made her thankful she only worked with canines. Dogs were trainable, but cats were another story altogether.

"I'm sure you had it all under control. Anyway, I know this is short notice, but I was hoping you could do me a big favor."

"What's in it for me?"

"My undying love and affection?"

"Already got that. What else?"

Miranda laughed. "Pub pizza, my treat. You say when."

"I'm all yours."

"That was easier than I thought. You should have held out." Penny laughed and Miranda continued, "Colin and I are getting away for the weekend, and I need someone to watch the dogs. They should be okay here. They'll be locked in the back, so if you can stop by in the morning and evening, walk them, feed them, pet them a little—you know the routine—that would be great."

"No problem. Will Rufus be staying there with Chuck and Lucy?"

"Yeah, he's been here most of the time, anyway.

The three of them are starting to be like a little family. He's doing so well. Anyway, Colin should be here soon and we'll be back sometime Sunday afternoon."

"A weekend trip, huh? That's romantic. Things are getting pretty serious, I take it?"

"Yeah, I suppose."

"But you still haven't told him the truth?"

"I've tried—I really have. I keep meaning to, but the time is never right, and with the harassment case, and—"

"Hey. It's all right. I understand, Randi. I'm not trying to make you feel guilty. I just hope it works out for you, I really do. You guys are good for each other."

Miranda was unsure what to make of Penny's change in attitude. Must be Travis was softening her up.

"Um, thanks. You know your opinion means a lot to me, Pen. It's just getting more complicated as time passes."

She could hear the smile in Penny's voice when she responded. "Yeah, tell me about it."

"Things with Trav are okay now? Did you guys talk?"

It was Penny's turn to sigh. "Yeah, they are. Things are great, in fact. I still think he's crazy, but for now I am willing to go with it."

"The sex is that good, huh?"

Penny laughed and Miranda was glad to lighten the tenor of their conversation.

"Yeah, actually, it is."

"Then I'm even more glad for you." She heard a car

pull into the driveway, and looked toward the window. "Pen, I hate to run, but Colin's here."

"Where are you going?"

"Not sure. We're going to pick a direction and see where we end up."

Penny laughed. "That's fun. Well, I hope you find somewhere nice."

"Thanks, I'll see you Sunday."

"Have a good time and no worries, the poochies are safe with me."

"I know. Thanks." Miranda hung up the phone just as Colin walked through the front door, Rufus at his side. He set Rufus free to join Chuck and Lucy while he proceeded to greet Miranda with a hot, long kiss. Her face was flushed when he pulled back.

"My, Professor Jacobs. You do know how to say hello."

He looked down at her, smiling, his eyes warm though there was strain in his expression, as well.

"I'm eager to get going—are we ready?"

"Just have to herd the dogs out back, then we're off. We probably have about six or seven hours of daylight, so we'll drive and then find somewhere to stay?"

"Sounds like a good plan."

She petted all the dogs and spoke to them softly before closing the door to the enclosed back porch. They would stay there and be able to run in and out to the yard through the built-in dog door she had installed when she moved in. Turning to go, Miranda stopped for a moment and raised her hand to Colin's cheek. She was picking up a definite vibe.

"Are you okay? You seem a little tense. Are you sure you want to go? We could stay here and..."

He leaned in and kissed her forehead. "No, I definitely want to go. I want to get out of here, and I want to be alone with you."

"Bad morning?"

"Nothing in particular. I spoke with the lawyer on the phone. They're going to look into it and contact me next week for an appointment."

Miranda nodded. "Let's go, then. We can talk more in the car."

Colin shifted uncomfortably. "Um, babe, do you mind if we don't? I'd like to talk—just not about that. I really want to try to put it out of my mind."

Miranda smiled gently. "Absolutely, whatever you want." The way she spoke the words triggered a responsive heat in his eyes, and she felt the thrill run all the way to her toes.

"Really? Whatever I want?"

She sent a playfully suspicious look in his direction, then locked the door.

"You have something specific in mind?"

Colin squeezed her hand as they walked to the car. "Many, many specifics. Shockingly detailed thoughts, even." He slid a veiled glance in her direction and leaned in to speak to her in a lowered voice. "Did you, uh, pack the vibrator?"

Miranda swallowed deeply. "It's in my bag."

They got into the car and she felt her sense of anticipation sharpen. It seemed as if they really were on the same wavelength. If all went well, this would be a weekend that neither one of them would forget.

COLIN RAISED his hand to his eyes and rubbed them hard. His vision was blurry and his head hurt. What the hell was going on? He looked around, recognizing Miranda's apartment. His gaze traveled to the table where there was a half-empty bottle of champagne and plump, red strawberries piled in a sparkling silver bowl.

Miranda was sitting on her bed in that sexy ivory lace gown he was always dreaming about. Her face was in her hands and her shoulders were shaking. He realized she was crying. But as he stepped forward to go to her, she raised her face to his, her eyes so full of pain he stopped in his tracks, a sense of dread overwhelming him.

"Randi, what's wrong? Let me help."

"Stay, and give us a chance, Colin, or just get out. It's your choice." Her voice caught, and she pressed her hand to her mouth, obviously fighting for control.

He stood helplessly for a moment, unsure of what to say, and then turned away. He didn't want to go— *why was he walking away?* She needed him, but he couldn't say anything or change his actions. A feeling of being trapped, unable to control his physical movements increased his panic. He turned the doorknob, stopping for a second as he heard her faint, ragged whisper a second before the door clicked shut.

"Fine, then. Just go."

Colin burst awake from the dream, his head splitting.

Momentarily disoriented, he looked around and saw Miranda sleeping next to him. Snoring lightly, she didn't seem disturbed by his movements.

The pounding in his head lessened a bit and he fell back onto the pillows, suddenly realizing the crashing sounds he thought were caused by his headache were actually coming from outside. Surf was slapping up onto the rocks not far from their window.

He relaxed as he remembered where he was. They'd driven up the coast, and it'd been great. He didn't even pay attention to how long they'd been in the car, listening to music, laughing and sometimes just sharing a companionable silence. He knew they were near the Acadia National Park, having spent many a vacation there as a child.

His breathing calmed and his muscles relaxed as he realized he'd just been caught in some horrible dream. He was here, with Miranda. Turning toward her, he touched her, making sure he was right, and that *this* wasn't the dream. Her warm flesh was smooth under his hands, and relief surged through him.

They had come across a beautiful inn right on the shore with first-rate rooms at off-season prices. The room was gorgeous, the bed huge. Colin remembered building a fire, and they'd ordered food in and made love long into the night until they'd both fallen into exhausted sleep.

Most of the time dreams were just dreams— accumulated images and emotions from the day that got jumbled up in sleep. Other times they were the means by which the brain worked out problems that were unsettling or unsolved. He grappled with the images and the emotions that had been so strong in his sleep, a sense of anxiety surfacing as he remembered walking away from her. His train of thought was broken by her fingers brushing across his face.

"Morning." She was studying him. He looked into her still-sleepy eyes, feeling love overwhelm him. No, he would never walk away from her, and nothing on earth could make him do so.

"Hey. I thought you were sleeping."

"I was. I don't think I've ever slept better in my life."

He cuddled her, rubbing his mouth over hers.

"Me, either. We do a nice job tiring each other out."

She smiled as her hands snaked lower, gliding over the soft hair on his stomach and past his waistline, finally curling around his warm, velvety erection. "You can say that again. We do a nice job waking each other up as well."

Colin laughed and stretched, pushing into her silken grasp. His headache was completely forgotten, the dream erased from his mind. "You're particularly talented at both tiring me out and waking me up."

"Mmm. You feel so good. I opened my eyes, and there you were. I just wanted to touch you. It's nice. To find you there."

"How long were you awake?"

"Only a few minutes. Long enough to see you were thinking hard about something serious, and so I thought

I would distract you. This weekend isn't about thinking, especially about unpleasant things, remember?"

Her sharp, white teeth nibbled down on his shoulder, then she began to feather kisses along his jaw, throat and chest, finally taking one of his flat, brown nipples between her teeth. She flicked her tongue over it, drawing out another moan from him. He would have thought they had spent all their passion last night, but with her it seemed endless.

"Thinking is vastly overrated."

She darted her tongue out, tasting his skin and licking a path lower to where her hand had been. Pushing the covers back, she slid down into a more comfortable position and wasted no time taking him completely into her mouth, loving him with lips and tongue and teeth until he was shuddering beneath her. Her hands traced a journey from his calves to his stomach, lighting on the sensitive spots in between. She scraped her nails over his hot skin in the secret places she knew would drive him insane.

"I...ohh, Randi...wait...."

She lifted, turning her head to face him, the ends of her hair tickling the places her mouth had just been. She looked at him with heated eyes and a playful pout that made his stomach flip. She started to turn back to him, but his hand on her shoulder stopped her.

His voice was a sexy whisper. "Come here."

She started to move toward him, but he shook his head and smiled. "Your mouth can stay there. I want the rest of you up here."

She moaned with instant appreciation and shuffled around, carefully straddling his shoulders, her heart beating madly now that his intent was clear. Leaning down over him again, she was enclosed by the dark curtain of her hair as it fell forward, his musky smell intoxicating her as she flicked her tongue over the sensitive skin of his sac, her anticipation of what he would do next pushing her desire to new heights.

She moaned in delighted approval as his tongue trailed along the inside of her thigh. He reached down and tweaked her stiff nipples as he bit and licked her tender skin. His mouth hadn't touched her yet—not where she longed to have him—and the thought of it drove her crazy. She sucked him hard, urging him on.

"Hold on there, sweetheart. We're taking it slow this time. I have a few surprises in store for you."

She nipped the head of his cock teasingly. If he was going to make her suffer, she would happily do the same for him. Somewhere in the back of her passion-soaked mind she wondered what surprises he was talking about, but didn't bother to think about it much more when his hands moved between her legs and opened her, his mouth fusing to her sex, lapping and prodding her until she almost screamed with the waves of pleasure she was feeling.

He took her to just the edge over and over again, flicking his tongue against her while he massaged her pulsing, delicate sweet spots with his fingers. Then he would draw back, keeping her suspended in taut anticipation, begging him to push her over, though she didn't beg with her voice. They were developing an entirely new, more intense way of communicating. His gasp answered her moan. Her cry echoed his growl. And then another sound entered the din, and she froze, everything still in the moment. The soft hum of her vibrator filled the air.

"Colin…?" She was breathing so heavily his name came out in a gulp.

He responded by edging down a bit lower, positioning himself so he could still get his mouth on her while he…*oh my*…her back arched as a burst of sensation rippled through her when he slid the vibrator, warmed by his hands, made slick by her own wetness, inside of her, all the while sucking and licking her swollen flesh. Pushing back, she rolled her hips, seeking release, her body shaking with the need for it. But then he withdrew again, rubbing it along her sex, over the secret pleasure points of her bottom, until she was sure she would pass out.

She couldn't think anymore. She wanted to come so desperately, but somehow she managed to keep herself poised above him. The teasing was over now. She ringed her forefinger and thumb tightly around the base of him, pulling down slightly, drawing the skin tight and making him bulge upward. She moved her fingers in short, hard strokes while encompassing him with her mouth. Drawing and pumping, swishing her tongue over him, he started to tremble, his limbs extended, his body bowed tight. Now they were definitely speaking each other's language.

She whimpered as he slid the gently pulsing instrument inside of her again. His mouth was no longer on her as she heard his own gasps and moans of pleasure, but his thumb massaged her intimately as the vibrator moved in and out, more deeply and more quickly with each passing moment, reflecting the speed of her mouth and hands on him almost perfectly. As if by design, they exploded in pleasure, their cries of rapture melding together as they were both consumed.

She sighed against the skin of his lower belly, resting her cheek against his thigh for a moment before she scooted up next to him, cuddling into his shoulder.

"My word, Colin. You do have some brilliant ideas. Feel free to surprise me more often."

He kissed her hair, his breathing still ragged, the scents of sex and the heat of their bodies hanging heavily in the room. "They're all inspired by you."

She laughed and he pulled back, looking down into her face, her cheeks still flushed with pleasure. "Really, Randi, with you, everything is different. I am literally flooded with ideas of things I want to do with you. To you." His voice dipped low, and her cheeks tinted a little more, her eyes sparkling.

She kissed him, smiling softly. "I've never shared things like this with anyone else either and I don't know if I would've been able to. With you, well… I trust you. I want to be completely open with you. Always tell me what you want."

"I will if you will. I love you."

"I love you, too." She drew the words out, enjoying the way they floated up from her heart.

He smiled, leaning down to kiss her nose. "How about we go in search of breakfast?"

"Sounds good." She fluttered her eyelashes in mock innocence. "Of course, we'll have to shower first."

Sitting up, he laughed and grabbed his pillow, socking her softly in the head with it. "Woman, you are insatiable. I think you've finally done me in, at least for a while, but if you are feeling up to the challenge, feel free to give it your best shot."

Following him into the bathroom, she grinned widely, watching his marvelous buttocks with sheer female appreciation. That's exactly what she had every intention of doing.

NORTHERN MAINE WAS greeting spring in its own peaceful fashion. The place was vastly different off-season, absent of tourists and the ever-present sportsmen and adventure seekers who frequented the trails, towns and waters during the summer months. Now it was largely locals who walked their dogs along the rocky headlands. Most of the shops, parks and tours wouldn't be open for another month or so. There was a sense of being outside of time, moments measured by the slow pace of your walk, the long roll of the waves into shore.

Colin inhaled the cool, damp sea air. Miranda walked by his side, her fingers loosely woven with his. They had picked up a disposable camera at the variety store and were taking pictures of each other as they strolled through the still-slumbering towns and along the rocky coastline. They had been walking all day, but he wasn't in the least bit tired; in fact, he felt completely renewed.

"We don't have one of us."

"Hmm?" Miranda looked out over the water at the seemingly endless numbers of migrating ducks. They had been lucky enough to spot some red-throated loons as well as the common loons that were seen more frequently.

There was nothing common about these birds, as far as Colin was concerned. Both variations of the bird were lovely—with their dramatic feather patterns, sharp eyes and haunting calls. *Loon* was such a comical name for such a beautiful bird. Colin had loved watching them since he was a child. He had even collected several art pieces that featured the lovely loons.

"We only have a few pictures left, and we haven't gotten one of us together. I don't know how we could work that out, though."

Miranda pointed to two young people walking toward them on the beach.

"Let's see if they can help." She jogged off, catching up with the couple in the distance. Soon, the three met Colin halfway in between. Miranda was flushed and sparkling from her short jog in the cool air. The young couple couldn't be much more than twenty years old, and were obviously crazy about each other.

"Cindi and Sean said they would shoot a couple pictures of us if we can get one of them, and we can mail it to them later."

Colin handed the camera to Sean. "Great! How about you get one or two of us here by the water, and then we'll switch and get you."

The photo session was fun, with Miranda sneaking her fingers up to make bunny ears behind Colin's head in the first shot while he grabbed her and dipped her into a low, dramatic kiss for the second picture. The young couple laughed at their antics then handed back the camera, and posed for their own picture, their faces shining as they gazed into each other's eyes rather than at the camera. When they were finished, they exchanged addresses and walked off into the sunset. Colin and Miranda stood for a moment, watching them.

"Jeez, they were so cute. All bright and shiny. Just think, we were that young once."

Colin laughed ruefully. "C'mon, it wasn't *that* long ago. Besides, you make me feel all bright and shiny." He rubbed his nose playfully on hers. She smiled up at him.

"Sometimes it feels like forever."

He wrapped his arm around her and they headed back to the car. He sensed a change in her mood and didn't say anything, letting whatever she wanted to say rise to the surface on its own. He simply squeezed her affectionately.

"I guess I was just wondering what it would be like now, if we had gotten together then. When we were that young."

Her comment hit him oddly, a mix of emotions keeping him from saying anything for several moments as he remembered all the times he had wanted to be with her but hadn't had the nerve or the opportunity to speak up.

"I'm sorry. I didn't mean to get all morose on you." Her face was turned up to his, her eyes studying him intently, and he smiled for her benefit in spite of the mix of emotions her comment had triggered. When they were almost back to the car, he led her to a bench near the parking area that looked out over the estuary. It was late afternoon and the sun was low, glinting on the water.

"No need to be sorry. I wonder how things would have been different, too."

She nestled against his shoulder. "Like if I hadn't dated Derek?"

He sighed, hating that she had brought it up. But they had to talk about it sometime. Derek had been an important part of both of their lives. He slipped his hand into her hair, rubbing soft strands between his fingertips.

"Yeah. I was furious when Derek went out with you. I wanted to flatten him when he told me he'd asked you out."

"You're kidding! You two fought?"

"Yeah. Well, I only got in one punch before Dad came out and broke it up, but you know, he got there first. I had to suck it up."

"I can't believe you actually fought about me."

He smiled at her surprised tone and slipped his hand out of her hair as she shifted forward on the bench, her attention fixed on his face.

"Why didn't you ever say anything?"

He shrugged. "I was young and stupid, and I didn't know what I really wanted until someone else had it. I think I was angrier with myself for not making a move than I was at him for being brave enough to do it."

"Brave? Was I so scary?"

"Petrifying. You were my friend, nothing more. Then, suddenly, I began to see you differently and had all these unexpected feelings." He smiled thinly and his regret showed in his eyes. "But there was also nothing that I could do about it. When you came back from Denver it hit me like a brick wall that I was still attracted to you—more than attracted. What I felt then was only a childish shadow of what I feel now."

"I know, me, too. So why didn't you say something?"

"You were my brother's girl—untouchable."

"Hardly. As you know, I wanted very much for you to touch me."

Heat flared in his eyes as he looked at her, but a slight edge of hardness glinted there as well. "No man wants to be second choice, Randi. Though for you, I was almost tempted to put my pride aside."

Miranda didn't say anything and he touched her face, looking at her inquisitively.

"What are you thinking?"

She wrapped her arms tightly around her, rising

from the bench to walk a few feet away, still staring out at the water. When he came up behind her and turned her around to face him, he was taken aback to find tears staining her cheeks. Suddenly his dream came crashing back to him. He pushed it out of his mind, and focused on her, right now, this moment.

"Honey, what happened? Why are you crying?"

She sniffed indelicately and shook her head, her voice breaking. "You were never second choice, Colin. I made a horrible mistake back then. I went out with Derek on a lark. I thought it would make you jealous. He didn't know that, though I think afterward he might have suspected. Maybe that's why he picked a fight with you—to see if you were interested. Then he died."

"Shh…it's okay. I know." But he didn't know. He wanted to comfort her, but his mind was scrambling to make sense out of what she'd just said, to make sure he had heard correctly.

She shook her head, wrestling out of his grip.

"No, you *don't* know. It's not your fault we lost all that time together—it's mine."

"It's no one's fault. It's just how things worked out. We're together now. That's what counts."

"Not entirely. We could have been together then, maybe if I had been brave enough to tell you the truth."

"About what?"

12

MIRANDA LOOKED UP into his face, her eyes drowning in his. "Oh, Colin. You're going to hate me for this." She looked down again, and he tipped her face up to his, shaking his head.

"Never. There's nothing you could do to make me hate you."

"You don't know that."

"I do. What happened with Derek?"

She took a deep breath. "He and I had split up. In fact, we broke up just a few hours before he had his accident."

Colin went stock-still. Miranda had broken up with Derek right before he died? His mind raced to process the information.

"You…broke up with Derek?"

She sniffed again, her eyes moist with tears. "Yes. Well, actually we broke up with each other. But I swear, he wasn't upset in the least. We even laughed about it. I guess he never had a chance to tell you."

"Why didn't you tell me?"

"I wanted to. But when he was killed, well, it wasn't

the kind of thing you say under those circumstances. And everyone was so upset, and I thought, that, um…." She kicked at the sand by her feet, looking away. "I thought you would all blame me, that everyone would think I upset him and caused the accident. And then I would have to admit that we never really had much romance between us, that I had just been trying to make you jealous, and then our friendship…well, it just seemed easier to let it go, except that it didn't go away. Everyone kept talking about Derek and me like we were still a couple. Even more so after he was gone."

"Especially me," he said, realization dawning.

"Well, yeah. I mean, I guess it was a natural assumption on everyone's part, but by the time it became a problem it was too late to tell everyone the truth. I was a coward."

He paused for a long moment and shook his head. "No, you were young. We all were. So you didn't stay away from home for so long because you were grieving? Heartbroken?"

"No. I mean, I was sad, of course, but I left for school because I needed to be out on my own, to find what it was I wanted to do." She paused for a moment, considering. "Though maybe I was avoiding dealing with the situation and the feelings I had for you were more than I could admit. I guess I thought they would go away if I wasn't here."

"And you were trying to make me jealous?" His voice was incredulous as he thought through all the things she had told him.

The emotions in her eyes communicated everything he needed to know.

He turned away, walked a few feet and turned to face her again. "But no one would have blamed you. It was always clear that Derek had no part in the accident. The car that hit him came out of nowhere. There was nothing he could have done. It wouldn't have mattered if he was distracted or not. The end result would have been the same."

"I know that now. I thought I was doing the right thing then. I never imagined you had any feelings for me. Other than friendship, that is." She looked at him. "I felt so bad about Derek. I didn't love him, but I liked him, and I felt guilty."

"Guilty? You had no reason to feel guilty."

"I did. Because I used him. I didn't think of it that way at the time, but that's what it amounts to. And even then, while we were mourning him, I could only think about you. How I was attracted to you, how I wanted to be there for you. But you were so devastated. How could I tell you what had happened? How would it have sounded for me to tell everyone Derek and I had just broken up when he was dead? And then there was no way to let you know I really wanted to be with you."

Colin nodded, sadness and understanding in his eyes, as he squeezed her shoulder.

"I guess I wouldn't have responded too well to that at the time."

"Understandably." She stared out over the water. "I figured leaving for school would help, you know, getting away, meeting other people. And it did work, until I came back."

He drew her to him. Burying his face in her hair as dusk surrounded them, he held her close. Finally, he stepped back and took her face in his hands.

"We did waste a lot of time, didn't we? With all our misperceptions and secrets."

She nodded. "I guess even now, I wonder, you know, if it's all settled."

"What do you mean?"

"I worry that you might regret being with me because you know, I, um, pushed this on you." She tested the ground by telling a half-truth and gauged his reaction.

His face was shadowed in the twilight, but his eyes were burningly intense, fixed on hers. What she saw there gave her hope.

"I loved my brother, Randi. I felt like I lost a part of myself when he died. And maybe I knew, deep down, that when he died, in a way I had lost you, too, because how could I tell you how I felt without betraying him? At least if he hadn't died maybe we would have all been honest about our feelings eventually, but it looks like you and I were in the same double bind. But now we're out of it, and I intend to stay that way."

"I don't think he would have felt betrayed. Like I said, he and I were only friends, and he loved you so much. I think he would be happy."

Colin nodded slightly. "I'd like to think that's true. And all that really matters is that we are together now. And I don't plan on letting you go."

Relief and happiness overwhelmed her, and the small voice at the back of her mind prodded, *tell him the rest of it, Miranda. Tell him.*

Miranda stared at him, tears flooding her eyes and flowing down her cheeks. She didn't say a word as she slid her arms around his neck, holding him as closely as she could, trying to find the courage to tell him everything, but she was too afraid of losing him now that they had come so far.

"I love you so much, Colin. Whatever happens, don't ever forget that."

"We've taken a long road to being together, but nothing is going to get in our way now. I promise."

Miranda closed her eyes tightly, blocking out her doubts and fears and focusing on how safe and good she felt in his arms. Maybe he was right. Maybe it would all work out just fine.

TRAVIS SMILED as he pushed through the heavy double doors of the hospital's pediatric wing. He was even happy for the steady sheet of rain that was going to soak him regardless of his raincoat, because it meant his car had conked out again and he was able to call Penny for a ride. She was there, waiting in her sleek little Subaru as she promised she would be. In return for the ride, he had promised her dinner, but in truth he was hoping for more.

He knew that beyond anything, he wanted to share his life with her. Working with kids in pediatrics for the past week had stirred his paternal instincts and he'd caught himself daydreaming about Penny pregnant with his child. His heart nearly burst at the very thought. He wanted everything with her. Now he had to convince her that they could have it all, together.

He didn't dare mention children right now or she would freak for sure. He'd been taking tiny steps, breaking down her doubts about what it meant to be married to a doctor, and so far his plan was working. She'd become much more relaxed and happy with him in the past few days. It was the perfect time, he thought, to take things one step further.

Opening the car door, he got in and, before she could even say a word, he covered her mouth in a hot, open-mouthed kiss that she responded to with equal desire, but then she was laughing and pushing playfully at him.

"Hey…cut it out. You're all wet."

"Are you?"

Penny laughed again and put the car in Drive, shaking her head at his naughty double entendre. Travis watched her in the dim light of the vehicle. Her taste lingered on his lips and he felt renewed determination to secure their relationship, to have Penny in his life permanently.

He knew her upbringing had created some major insecurities that still ate away at her confidence, but he was working on that, though he was feeling less patient than usual. They'd wasted too much time already. He turned to face her and took the leap.

"Pen, I want to ask you out on a date."

"Huh?" Her eyes were glued to the road and she

wasn't really listening, still warm from his kiss and caught up in thought about the man sitting next to her. That was happening a lot lately. Just the thought of Travis or a simple touch, a kiss, and her body and heart slammed into high gear.

The delicious taste of his kiss mingled with the sweetness of the rain sent her straight to heaven in about two seconds flat. She loved how much fun he was. Even when it came to sex, he was always surprising her. She wiggled in her seat, the damp warmth of her desire evident as she thought about him.

He was quiet again until they pulled into the parking lot of the restaurant where they had agreed to have dinner. As she shut off the car, she turned to him, answering his question now that she could give him her full attention.

"A date? Isn't that what we're on now?"

"This is not a date. This is pasta."

"Two people out for dinner is a date."

"Not in my book."

"Okay, so what does your book say?"

He moved nearer but didn't touch her, making her pulse zip. He smiled mysteriously.

"Well, a date includes flowers, dressing up, and doing something that we don't just do in the usual course of a day. It's special, something out of the ordinary. Romantic, even."

Penny smiled, but suddenly wanted to deflect this course of conversation and go to dinner. "Anything I do with you is romantic, Trav."

Travis's joy at her sweet comment was clear in his eyes, but he wasn't to be distracted so easily. He tipped his forehead close to hers. "I do believe you just said something very nice to me, Pen. It makes me all fluttery inside." He smiled broadly, and she smiled back, and they both felt the warmth of the moment building between them.

"But as nice as it is to know you feel that way, I would like to take you somewhere fancy. To a hospital event next Friday night."

She felt herself tense immediately. Why would he ask her to do this? He knew she didn't do fancy. She didn't even own a fancy dress, she couldn't afford one, and she wouldn't buy one if she could. It just wasn't her style. She pulled away from him physically and emotionally, sitting back in her seat and forcing her voice to be casual.

"Look, I'm starving, let's go in. The rain seems to be stopping."

"Not yet. I want you to come to this party with me, Penny. It's important."

She closed her eyes and fought for patience, knowing she wasn't going to get to dinner unless she talked this out, but she felt trapped, and repressed the desire to bolt from the car.

"Travis, you know I'm not comfortable at those types of events. I don't have fancy clothes and I don't know how to mingle with those kinds of people."

"What kinds of people?"

"You know, muckety-mucks, big shots, important

people. You know how uncomfortable that makes me and I thought you respected that."

"Oh, no, this is about you, not me. And no, I don't respect the fact that you have a lower opinion of yourself than you should. You absolutely can mingle with *those* kinds of people, and maybe you'd even enjoy it. How do you know? You've never tried, have you?"

She shrugged. "I can imagine. And what would they think of you, being with someone—"

"What? Someone beautiful, smart and interesting, not to mention fun, sexy and just generally wonderful? They are hardworking people going out for a night to have some fun and for a good cause. The proceeds from the dinner go to the Children's Burn Unit. C'mon. We'll have fun."

She shook her head, knowing she was being mulish, but not able to face her fear. Then she jumped when Travis nudged his face into the crook of her neck and kissed her gently below her ear, and whispered, "Still hungry?" before he began doing evil things to her neck with his tongue. She shivered, losing track of her thoughts, and tipped her head a little, giving him better access. When he tugged her collar down and dragged his tongue across her collarbone, she forgot all about food and anything else.

"No."

"No what?"

"Not hungry…don't stop doing that, oh…but you're not going to trick me into going to that party with you."

Travis's breath heated her skin as his hand slipped

under her raincoat and massaged her breast through her shirt. Excited tremors shot through her when he pinched her distended nipple and she wondered what the heck was it with them and cars? But with the delicious things he was doing to her, she really didn't care where they were. The windows were fogged and no one could see.

"No, no tricks, maybe some bribery though…."

She didn't really get his meaning at first, until his mouth closed over hers and he slid the zipper of her jeans down, easing his hand inside to where she was slick and ready.

"Trav! Oh…." She was amazingly, immediately hot and ready. If he would just touch her, she could…*ohh*. That's what he meant by bribery. No way! No way would he dare be so manipulative. She shifted around, seeking his hand and finally put her own over his, trying to show him what she needed.

But he knew. He just wasn't going to give it to her. He bent down and the moment before he pressed his mouth against the hot flesh of her exposed tummy, he whispered, "Come to the party with me, Pen, please."

She shook her head wordlessly, fighting the need he was stoking within her. His fingers were sliding against her, his mouth dancing over her skin everywhere and landing on her breast, suckling her through her bra until she whimpered pathetically.

He raised his head to watch her. His fingers finally moved. He slid one slowly inside her heat and she lifted, trying to thrust against him, but he just rubbed her lightly, teasingly, then withdrew.

"Come with me, Penny."

"This isn't fair." She could feel release just seconds away, if he would help her a little bit. He flicked his thumb over her swollen nub once, and she bit her lip, groaning his name in frustration. His voice became lower, more urgent.

"Come with me, Pen. Say yes."

He won. She felt weak and pathetic, and somewhere in her head she was pretty pissed off, but she was willing to do just about anything right now if he would just finish what he started.

"Okay. Okay. Fine. I'll go to the stupid party. Now—"

He stopped touching her all together, and her eyes flew open in protest. His face was close to hers, his eyes making passionate promises.

"You mean it?" He slid inside again, one finger, then two....

"Yes! I'll go. Travis, *please.*"

Lights exploded behind her eyelids as he finally applied the quick thrust and pressure she was seeking. She ground against him, clenching, making it last. When it was over he withdrew his hand and kissed her. She thought she would be angry when the moment passed, mad at him for taking advantage of her, but the look on his face, the gratitude and deep emotion she saw there, made any anger she might have felt drift away. Oh, man, she loved him far too much for her own good.

She slanted a look sideways at him, smiling because she couldn't help herself. "Just don't say one word. Not one word."

He smiled at her, looking as innocent as the driven snow. "Hungry now?"

GETTING AWAY for the weekend had been just the ticket. The day had been perfect, and the night was even more so. Still, while they laughed, talked and made love, Colin couldn't help but sense something in the air between them. The edgy feeling he'd had when he'd first emerged from unconsciousness after his accident was back—that itching at the back of his mind, the sense that he was missing something. Even though he and Miranda had cleared the air about Derek, he couldn't quite rid himself of that uneasy feeling. There was a knot of anxiety in his chest that he couldn't loosen.

Turning his head, he looked at her in the moonlit darkness. Her dark hair was tumbled everywhere, her lips still swollen from endless kisses. Every time she told him she loved him—and every time he was able to tell her—his heart had a reason to keep on beating. So why wasn't he sleeping like a baby or relishing that life had given him this gift? He was finally with the woman of his dreams, and he was a mess. It made no sense.

Frustrated, he slipped out from under the down-filled comforter and put on his jeans and shirt. Walking out onto the small balcony, he shivered in the cold night air. He watched the white foam of the waves splash on the glistening edges of rock lit by the moon. Beyond the white foam of the shore, everything was blackness. Resting on the balcony rail, he tried to clear his mind.

He breathed in deeply, whispering a mantra he had learned in a meditation class he had taken years ago. Meditation, which meant "mind deliverance," generally helped soothe his restless thoughts or anxieties, but he rarely devoted the time to it that he should. Still, he practiced often enough to remember how to do it, and found it useful during particularly stressful times.

Lowering into a sitting position on the cold wooden slats of the balcony, he crossed his legs and placed his hands in the healing prayer position, chanting softly into the sea breeze.

"Om Mani Padme Hum...Om Mani Padme Hum...."

It was only a matter of minutes before he began to relax and his muscles started to unwind. He breathed evenly, the slosh of the waves becoming a background noise that eased into his consciousness, matching the pace of his slow chant. Falling more and more deeply into his relaxed state, he watched images pass before him, his thoughts becoming like objects floating away on the breeze, leaving his mind in peace.

Fatigue crept up on him and he stopped chanting, releasing himself from the meditation while still maintaining his relaxed state so that he could go to bed and finally sleep. But as he rose, a strange, foggy feeling hit him. He swore, feeling dizzy, and grabbed the railing, trying to get his bearings. He raised his face, looking through the glass doors where Miranda was still sleeping in the darkness, wondering if she would hear him if he called for help, but then everything righted itself again, and he stood up straighter.

Memories flooded back like the tide washing in and he suddenly remembered the night of his accident as clearly as if it had just happened.

Everything became clear. The dream he'd had that morning was not really a dream at all—it'd been a memory. He wasn't sure what to do. Numbly he turned and stepped back inside the room. Relief mixed with confusion and anger. He hadn't harassed Nell that evening, and he also hadn't made love with Miranda.

All this time he had doubted himself, beating himself up for harassing Nell, leaving Miranda after making love to her. Now he saw the lies as well as the truth. Trying to control the emotions coursing through him, he found the small sofa by the TV and sat, his head in his hands.

Miranda had tried to seduce him; that much was true. The image of her crying on the side of the bed came back to him like a fist in the gut. And yes, he *had* left her, but without succumbing to her. He had been too unsure, too convinced that what they had couldn't work. Too choked by his doubts. He sucked in a painful breath and tried to process it all.

Why would Miranda tell him that they'd had sex when they hadn't? He looked toward the bed, and knew, his heart aching. She had played him. She knew if he thought they'd slept together once, the door was open for it to happen again.

And he'd felt so guilty about leaving her. He recalled his thoughts standing by the rail in Old Port before the bike slammed into him. He'd hated hurting her, but did it justify her actions? He'd told her nothing could come between them, but the fact that she'd lied to him so blatantly stung deeply.

His head was swimming and he wanted answers. He opened his mouth, intending to wake her up, to demand an explanation, but something held him back. He was furious with her, but he also loved her.

The fact that he loved her didn't just go away because these new thoughts and feelings had exploded in his head. And he'd never been her second choice. But what chance did their relationship have if it was built on lies? On the fact that she was obviously *willing* to lie to him to get what she wanted?

He'd never have thought that of her. She'd taken advantage of him in a very weak state. But while on one hand her actions were reprehensible, his gut clenched at the thought of losing her. And considering their talk earlier, he could almost understand. Almost, but not quite.

He stood and took a step toward the bed, his heart battling with his mind. What would he do? She'd said, several times, that she needed to talk with him, that she had something to tell him. Was she going to tell him the truth? Would she have told him eventually? But when?

Wide-awake again, he considered his options carefully. He didn't want to lose her, but he also wanted the truth. She said she loved him, but how far would she have let it go? Could she really love him and still live a lie? Unable to return to the bed, he sat quietly in the dark, having no idea what to do next.

13

"YOU LOOK STUNNING."

Penny wrinkled her nose and looked down at the swath of midnight-blue silk wrapped around her curvy form, exposing slender shoulders and a glimpse of leg each time she moved. Glancing in the mirror, her eyes reflected her uncertainty and fears.

"I guess. It's a nice dress—it cost enough. I will have to live on peanut butter all next week."

Miranda crossed the room to hug her, then framed Penny's face with her palms. Penny was a vision. It had been such fun helping her shop for her dress and getting her all done up to go to the charity ball with Travis. The dress accentuated the ivory tone of her skin and made her eyes sparkle. Her red hair was pinned up in an elegant do, held with a diamond clip Miranda had lent her, and she wore a minimum of makeup. Just enough to transform her from merely beautiful to drop-dead gorgeous.

"It'll be worth it. You'll be lucky if Travis is even able to speak when he sees you." Color infused Penny's cheeks, and she bit her lip self-consciously.

"You think so? That's probably a good thing. Every time we talk, we get a little deeper into this thing. He has a way, I don't know, of making it seem like, like—"

"Like everything is going to be okay? Like things will work out?"

Penny sighed. "Yeah."

"And what's wrong with that?"

"Nothing. Everything. I don't know. I just wish I could be as sure about things as he is."

"Penny, Travis is a great guy. He's crazy about you. Just enjoy it. You look great. This is the kind of night that only comes around once in a while, so don't worry it into submission."

Miranda took Penny's shoulders and turned her to the mirror, both of their faces reflected back at them. "Look at you. You're amazing. You're smart, funny, kind and beautiful—how could Travis not love you? You're going to knock them dead tonight, don't worry."

"It's just all those strange people, and I'm not used to this kind of thing...."

"Doesn't matter. You have Travis, and he's the only one you have to worry about. Have some faith, Pen."

"If you say so," she said with a worried sigh.

"Oh, believe me, I'm getting to be an expert on the subject."

"What's that supposed to mean? Are things okay with you and Colin? You haven't mentioned him much this week."

Miranda stepped away, suddenly feeling unsure of

how to answer. It had been a busy week, or so Colin told her, what with exams coming up and dealing with the sexual harassment case. She'd hardly seen him. He'd spoken with the lawyers and she knew they'd set up a face-to-face meeting to discuss the situation. She wanted to be there to support him, but he seemed very distant all of a sudden.

She knew Colin needed to address these issues in his life, and that he was under a lot of stress and busy at work, but she missed him horribly. It was disconcerting to realize how important he'd become in her life after being out and on her own, not depending on anyone, for so many years.

But it wasn't as if she was just sitting around twiddling her thumbs, either, though. Business was picking up and there'd been a lot to do getting Penny ready to go to the party. But deep down she could feel the wall cementing between her and Colin. Even worse she had no idea why it was there.

Maybe their talk about Derek had made him reconsider. Maybe he had been caught up in the moment. When she mentioned it, he had kissed her and apologized for being distracted by work. It made her feel like a neurotic idiot, but she didn't feel any better, any more comforted by his excuses.

"I guess we're okay. Hard to know, since I haven't seen him much this week. I guess he's just been busy."

Penny arched an eyebrow doubtfully. "Too busy for you? I find that hard to believe."

Miranda shrugged. "There's been a lot going on.

He's trying to deal with the harassment case. It's a busy time of the term, and his parents are due back from their trip soon. We can't be together every minute." Even to her own ears, she sounded defensive and less than convincing.

"Are you going to talk to him?" About what didn't even need to be stated. Penny's meaning was clear.

Miranda felt the familiar tightness in her chest. "I have to. Things have gone too far to let it go any longer. I didn't really think that would happen—I guess I didn't really think too much at all. But I am going to do it, I promise. We have time set aside this weekend, and I'll tell him then."

It was clear that Colin's memory was not returning, and she knew she had to take the bull by the horns. He'd taken the news about Derek well, and she believed he loved her. If they were going to try to make something lasting out of this relationship, she had to tell him everything. She also had to accept there would be busy times, when everything was not wine and roses, without becoming a neurotic mess. She imagined it was her own guilt that was causing most of the problems.

True to the magazine article that had gotten her into this mess, the last step in her total seduction would be to *expose,* to share any hidden secrets, to bare herself to him, body and soul. Nothing could get in the way this time. She just hoped that when he learned the truth, the bond they had developed over the years and particularly the past few weeks, could withstand it.

Penny's gaze was sympathetic and she took both of

Miranda's hands in hers, squeezing them supportively. "Hey, have some faith. Someone smart told me that. Things will work out."

Miranda tried to smile. She sincerely hoped so.

COLIN WAITED PATIENTLY outside the dean's office, watching the late afternoon sun sparkle behind the large pines that edged the quad. When he heard footsteps in the hall, he knew he was ready to take care of at least one of the misperceptions that had turned his life upside down of late. He remembered what had happened with Nell that night in his office, and while he still found it astounding that his intentions could've been so drastically misunderstood, at least now he could defend himself.

The only way to clear the air was to have an honest, face-to-face meeting with all parties involved and fortunately, after explaining his recovered memory to Dean Malcolm, that had been arranged. Now that he could recall what had happened that night, he felt more confident about putting the matter to rest.

When Nell walked into the waiting area with two of the lawyers, Colin tensed, but he forced himself to nod at Nell, saying a quiet hello. She looked terrible, pale and practically shaking with nerves. Regardless of the tension between them, his heart went out to her. Fortunately, the secretary buzzed the dean right away, and within minutes they were all seated facing each other in a circle in front of the desk. Dean Malcolm cleared his throat.

"The reason we've called this meeting is because Professor Jacobs has experienced a return of his memory."

The dean stopped speaking and turned to Colin, nodding, as everyone else's attention perked up as well, especially Nell's. "And now that we have a description of what happened that evening from both sides, I hope we can have a productive conversation."

Colin felt bolstered by the dean's confident, positive tone. Colin briefly acknowledged everyone, but made eye contact with Nell, specifically.

"Nell, I just need to ask a few questions, even though I recall what happened now. Is that okay?" Colin asked.

Nell looked at her lawyers, who nodded reassuringly, and then she made a vague gesture of assent toward Colin.

"Thank you. What specific things happened that made you feel uncomfortable that night?"

One of the lawyers started to speak, pointing out that everything was in the report, but Colin interrupted. "Please, I want Nell to tell me what I did exactly that made her feel uncomfortable, so I can compare it against what I recall. Even though my memory has come back, there could be gaps."

Nell clasped her hands tightly in her lap.

"I, um, mostly that you asked me out, and you put your arm around me."

Colin regarded her patiently, measuring his words carefully. "I do recall that, Nell, and I'm sorry that I may have been too familiar with you in that respect, but

I was only concerned that you were working very hard and you were fatigued. I can see how my gesture could have come across as being too friendly." Colin leaned forward, holding her gaze with his.

"I shouldn't have touched you in any way, though I meant no harm by it. I meant it only as a gesture of camaraderie. And yes, I did ask you out—for coffee—not on any kind of date, or with any romantic intention. Do you believe me?"

The young woman's eyes were guarded, her voice barely audible. "I just felt, that you...you said you wanted a different relationship with me than you had had with your advisor."

Colin closed his eyes, the pieces clicking together. How could he have been so stupid? He'd been tired that night, and he'd been distracted—by his interlude with Miranda, most obviously—and he hadn't taken care with his words in his rush to leave the office.

"That's true. I guess I should have told you that my advisor was a guy from the old school. He treated me like a slave, piled so much work on me I barely made it through the semester, and never spoke a friendly word. I swore the entire time I worked with him that if I was ever lucky enough to have a teaching assistant, I wouldn't abuse them that way. I wanted to make sure I wasn't making you think you had to work like a dog. I guess I ended up overcompensating in the other direction. But that's all it was, I swear. I wish you had talked to me about it."

Color rushed into Nell's cheeks and her eyes filled,

a fat tear dropping down her cheek. Colin grabbed a box of tissues from the dean's desk and handed them to her, waiting for her to speak, though he wasn't sure what to expect. If anything, she looked more miserable than she had before.

"I'm sorry, Professor Jacobs, I *couldn't* talk to you. I'm so confused…."

"Take your time, Nell. No one is angry here. It's going to be okay."

She nodded at him. "I feel so horrible now, what I did to you, but I didn't know what to do." Nell glanced around nervously. "I did like you, and you seemed so much nicer, and younger. Then I thought, maybe you were really interested, and maybe it would be okay, since I knew you weren't married…."

More tears fell, and Colin shifted a little but controlled his own awkwardness at her confession, letting her continue. "But then I came to your office that night, and you were with that woman, your friend. I knew that now it was just like before. You wanted to use me, I thought, anyway…."

Colin's internal radar perked up, sensing a marked increase in the level of her tension, like clouds gathering before a storm. "Before?"

He waited for Nell to catch her breath. "At my other school, where I did my master's. My advisor, he seemed to like me, too—you know, more than like me," she said, her head hanging down, her voice a low murmur. "We, um, got involved, and he took me out, and you know, things happened. Then he told me he was married, but he wanted me to keep seeing him, d-doing things with him, and when I said I wouldn't, he… threatened me with my assistantship. He said I had no proof he'd done it, and no one would believe me over him, so I had no choice."

Colin and everyone in the room were speechless with shock, and Nell's shoulders shook, her voice rising hysterically.

"I couldn't believe it was happening again. At first I thanked my lucky stars you were so nice to me, but then it changed, and I knew I couldn't let it—let anyone u-use me again like that." Her sobs started coming in gulps and Colin stood, worried she would pass out, "I—I had to tell someone…I thought there's something wrong with me, that I had this happen twice. I'm so sorry."

Colin crossed the space between them and knelt by Nell's side, his concern for her as she dissolved in tears overriding his worry about propriety. One look at the faces of the people around him and he knew they felt the same.

The dean nodded, his mouth set in a hard line. "We'll look in to it. For now, we'll consider this case settled?" The dean looked for the assenting nods from the lawyers, which he received. "And move forward with getting things back to normal." The dean buzzed his secretary, asking her to send for someone from the student counseling center to come to the office. "And Nell?"

The woman raised her head, peering up at the dean

in misery, obviously expecting the worst, but his voice was gentle.

"We'll work things out. Don't worry. Just get yourself feeling better, okay? We're here to help."

Nell nodded and stood, shaking, supported by Colin as the secretary entered the room and flanked her other side, leading her from the office. As the lawyers filed out, Colin excused himself to the secretary and closed the door behind, facing the dean.

"She's been through a lot. Too much. Do we have her former advisor's name?"

The dean nodded. "Yes. I'm going to check that out personally."

"Good. I'll do anything I can to help. And if Nell wants to be my T.A., I would be happy to work with her again—this wasn't her fault, and it must have been eating at her to keep it inside for so long." Colin shook his head in self-reproach. "I wasn't thinking clearly when I spoke to her that evening, and I want to apologize for that. It won't happen again."

"You can't monitor every word that comes out of your mouth, Colin, or know how someone else will hear it. It's your job to guide T.A.s, but nothing you did was so horribly out of line. You never can tell what's going on under the surface, though, can you?"

Colin's mouth twisted self-derisively. "I should have been more aware, more careful—"

"You can't predict everything. We'll make sure she gets appropriate help and she'll have a place here if she wants it. I'm sure your support will mean a lot to her.

I'm glad your memory came back or this might have never been discovered, and much more harm would have been done. To your career and to other young women whom this man could be victimizing."

The two men shook hands before Colin left. He hadn't revealed to anyone outside of the people in that room and Travis that his memory had returned. Travis was bound by doctor-patient confidentiality, which gave Colin control over how he let everyone know what was happening. The entire week had been topsy-turvy since his return from his weekend away. Life had changed completely—again—in just the space of a day.

Now he had to deal with Miranda. He'd been avoiding the issue for days, which didn't help much. It simply added missing her to the emotional tangle he was dealing with. He was angry with her, but he didn't want to risk losing her. If he confronted her on the issue, they might clear the air, but it might also end their relationship. How could he ever really, really trust her? Yet, how could he let her go?

Walking across the quad, the sunny weather cheered him and he watched campus life explode as it always did as the days became longer and warmer—Frisbees and softballs being tossed, classes being held outside, students sleeping in the sun. Sprouts of flowers poked up everywhere in the gardens, and some bright yellow daffodils already were in bloom. Everything was being renewed.

He stopped suddenly, standing in place, almost colliding with the people who were walking behind him. Another moment of clarity. He excused himself out of the way, stepping to the side, and knew he had found his answer. In order for him to know if their relationship stood a chance, he had to find out exactly how far Miranda was willing to take her lie. And he knew exactly how to do it.

PENNY TOOK A DEEP BREATH and opened the door. Miranda had been right. Travis couldn't speak. His eyes traveled over her, passion, awe and delight communicating themselves to her silently. She felt the same, seeing him dressed to the nines in his tux, holding a stash of red roses, which, after a few minutes of staring, he handed to her. As she took the flowers, he stepped forward, sliding his arms around her.

"Penny, you look…there are no words…beautiful is an understatement."

"You like?" She stepped back and twirled slowly for him, amazed at how the look on his face was triggering an answering excitement in her heart. All the uncertainty faded and she felt like a…woman. A desirable, gorgeous woman whose man was looking at her as if she was the beginning and end of all creation. Giddy, she felt energy bubble through her veins, and did an excited little hop, feeling a laugh emerge.

The warmth in Travis's eyes now, more than any other time, touched her to the core. His eyes were dead serious as he stared at her and she faltered for a second. But then he was there, bringing his mouth down on hers in such a way that she had no doubts about his feelings. The thick length of him nudged her thigh and she felt breathless, digging her fingers into his back as her knees buckled.

"We could just keep the party here." Her voice was husky and she looked up at him, the flush from his kiss warming her face.

He shook his head, his smile more handsome than ever.

"No way. We're going and I am planning to show you off to every person there."

Penny felt another giddy giggle threaten as he placed her wrap over her shoulders. Show her off? No one had ever talked about showing her off before. Suddenly she was looking forward to this evening very much. Miranda had been right—she should have faith and have fun. Travis was the only one who mattered.

COLIN TOYED with his steak, looking across the table at Miranda, who also didn't seem to have a huge appetite.

"You okay?"

She nodded, peering at him with what seemed to be a slight bit of apprehension in her eyes. They were supposed to be celebrating his settlement of the Nell problem, but things were awkward between them. He didn't like it.

He'd had to tell a slight lie about the meeting, saying that Nell had avoided taking any blame for the misunderstanding. So, on top of everything else, he had his own lies now. Things were getting too complicated. He was tempted to just call it even and say everything was okay and that they should forget it and move on.

But he knew that wasn't right, either. While he would always love her, he had to know if she would ever tell him the truth or if she would let the lie stay between them forever. If that was the case, what kind of life could they have? No, what he was doing was what he needed to do. Stretching his arm across the table, he wove his fingers with hers.

"I'm sorry I have been so out of it the last few days. I know I've been preoccupied."

She sighed, squeezing his fingers. "I know, me too. No apologies. It's been a weird week. Last weekend was wonderful, though. I couldn't have asked for a more perfect time."

"Yes, and though we haven't had much time together this week, I was hoping you might be willing to help me out with something."

Curiosity sparked in her eyes. "Sure. What?"

"Well, the memory loss is still really bugging me. Travis says my memory is not likely to come back since it hasn't done so on its own yet." He ignored the pinch of guilt that he felt with yet one more fib and continued, "But I was thinking, as a last-ditch effort, maybe we could stage, um, a reenactment."

She looked at him quizzically across the table. "A reenactment of what?"

"Of the evening I had my accident—from the point I can remember. I know I got your e-mail, and I must have come over, but what happened? What happened *exactly?* If we go through it all again, maybe it will jog something loose in my brain. Maybe I'll remember. But it would have to be exact." He pushed his plate back, focusing intently on her.

"How exact, exactly?"

"As close as possible. Any sights, smells or other physical sensations can trigger memory. I did a little research and sometimes these staged reenactments are worth a shot." He smiled, rubbing his thumb across the tender inside of her palm. "And if not, it will be a fun evening anyway. I would like to know what you did—what *we* did—that night. I hate having forgotten. You could seduce me all over again."

He watched her shift uneasily in her seat and felt the tightness in his chest increase. What was she thinking? He leaned forward, making his best plea, though on some level he felt like a dog doing it.

"Please, Randi. It would really help me to know we at least tried. Then if it doesn't work, I can try to put this to rest, and I will at least have some memory of the first night we shared together, even if it's not the actual first time."

Damn. She was stuck now. Hoisted by her own petard. Miranda had no idea what a petard was, but she knew hers had been hoisted. How could she possibly refuse his request? She could blurt out the truth now, but she'd hoped to do it under better, and possibly more forgiving, circumstances. Maybe he was handing her the perfect opportunity. Maybe she could do the reenactment—exactly as it happened—as a way of telling him. Suddenly the pieces clicked into place. Yes, that would be perfect.

She also knew that if he left her this time, as he had the first, she would be devastated. But he deserved the truth and her help in regaining his memory. She took a deep breath.

"Okay. Tomorrow night. Come over at eight. We'll do it…exactly as we did it that night."

He squeezed her hand. "Thank you. I know it may seem a little strange, but it could work."

She drew her hand away from his, picking up her fork. She'd taken a chance before and she was going to have to take one again. She hoped the night would go better this time.

ROSE PETALS WERE scattered everywhere. They were crushed in the bed, stuck to her skin, and even… *blech*…Penny peeled one from the side of her lip. Travis lay beside her, naked, gorgeous, and satisfied— for the moment. The evening had been one of the best of her life. She had received so many compliments on her dress she almost didn't know what to do. And Travis. He'd been incredible.

During the entire party, she swore he'd never taken his eyes from her, had plied her with champagne, proudly—*proudly*—had introduced her to his friends. She'd even met the director of the hospital board, who'd said Travis was one of their best doctors and that they should both come to his Fourth of July barbecue.

Penny had danced with Travis, secure in his arms, floating on his attentiveness, and had felt comfortable with the people she'd met. It'd been perfect.

When they'd returned home, he'd swung her up into his arms and had carried—actually *carried*—her into the bedroom where he'd proceeded, as her romance novels described it, to ravage her thoroughly. She grinned at the ceiling, loving that she finally knew what it felt like to be thoroughly ravaged. Her head fell to the side, her cheek resting on his shoulder, only to find he was still looking at her, that same adoring look in his eyes.

His skin was glistening with sweat from the energetic lovemaking they had engaged in. She slid her attention over him in the low light of her bedroom. There were sides to Travis she never would have dreamed existed, and each new discovery made her love for him stronger than ever.

She finally believed it could be possible. More than possible—it was a reality. He'd been absolutely right about making her attend the party. She hadn't felt out of place or less than anything or anybody. She'd even met some women who read the same books she did, enjoyed the same authors. As medical staff, they'd also seemed sincerely interested in her work at the vet's office, and she thought she had pulled off talking about her job rather brilliantly.

She grinned widely, thinking that could be the first time she had ever thought of herself as brilliant in any way whatsoever. It felt pretty damned good, too! A weight seemed to lift, and for the first time in her life she felt gloriously happy. With Travis she had felt like the queen of the world. Somehow she knew he would always make her feel that way.

"What are you thinking about?"

She ran the tip of her finger down the line of his straight nose, landing it on his lips, where he drew her finger into his mouth, creating new shivers of desire throughout her body.

"You. And me. And tonight."

"You were fantastic. Everybody loved you, but not nearly as much as I do."

Her heart did a funny little flip, and she raised up on one elbow, looking down into his eyes.

"I love you, too." She'd loved him for so long, and now she felt free to say it, to show it. Confidence made her daring. Tonight was truly magical and she wanted it to stay that way, forever.

Shock was quickly replaced with warmth and love as he gathered her close to him, rocking her back and forth.

"God, Penny, I've waited forever to hear you say that. I love you more than I can possibly ever tell you." His voice was muffled, but happy.

She smiled, her heart in her throat.

"Prove it," she said, her voice husky with passion, but teasing as well.

"How?"

"Marry me, Travis."

14

COLIN SECOND-GUESSED HIMSELF for the umpteenth time as he drove to Miranda's house for their "reen-actment." His stomach clenched. Maybe he should have come clean about his memory. Was it fair to test her like this? But then again, was it fair for her to have seduced him with lies? Maybe "fair" didn't have much to do with it. An orange sun was setting over the horizon when he pulled up in front of her house, but he was hardly paying attention to the beauty of it.

He stepped out of the car and forced himself to approach the front door, his doubts dogging him all the way. Knowing what to expect yet pretending he had no idea was *not* going to be easy. His mind was already flipping images of that first night in front of his eyes—Miranda in the ivory gown, Miranda kneeling by his side, her mouth touching him intimately as he watched in the mirror. Could he possibly pull this off?

When the door squeaked open, he pushed his hands into his pockets as he fought between nerves and desire. But then there she was, a perfect vision in ivory lace as he had seen her in his mind so many times since that fateful evening, her lush body poised before him, just as she had been then. He saw the hesitation in her eyes and he felt a stab of guilt.

Though his arousal had been clouded by anxiety up to that point, his blood rushed south at the sight of her. Reflexively, he started to speak, unsure exactly what was going to come out of his mouth, but she stopped him, playing by the rules. He wasn't supposed to speak.

"No. No talking. Just come in."

He stepped in, heard the door click shut behind him. He met her at the top of the stairs, as he had that evening, though he knew this time it was no joke.

Memories and reality merged and he swallowed, realizing she had met his request. The room looked exactly as he remembered. There was champagne chilling, strawberries piled in a bowl, and the bed was turned down. A weird déjà vu crept over him, and he felt his passion dip, but then she walked up to him and he felt his groin tighten immediately in response to her scent.

He couldn't speak. Sheer male instinct took over, and he was on fire, wanting her desperately. She was acting it out perfectly, not having missed a single detail. She was as beautiful as he remembered, maybe more so since he knew now what it was like to be with her, to love her fully.

"Mir—"

"Shh! No talking. I told you."

She was in charge—she had no doubts. He was as turned-on by her command of the situation now as he had been the first time. His body leaped in response as she stepped up close. Her breasts grazed his chest when she pushed the lightweight jacket from his shoulders and loosened the knot of his tie, which only made the blood pulse even harder through his veins.

She looked into his eyes, brazen and open in her desire, but there was something else there now, too—more warmth, love, and something uncertain. Fear, perhaps? The thought made him shift uncomfortably, but her sultry voice drew his attention back to her.

"I'm going to feed you."

Everything progressed as before, though he was sure he saw her hand tremble when she poured a glass of champagne and took a sip before she dipped a ripe strawberry into the glass and lifted it to his mouth. He took a bite, trying to catch the drizzle of juice that escaped down his chin.

The feeding went on for torturously long minutes. Had it lasted this long before? She not only fed him but let him watch her eat, which included her dipping her fingers into the champagne and tracing it down her chest, along the edges of the nightgown over the creamy curves of her breast. He wanted her badly, even though their situation was staged. That first night he had walked away. He didn't know if he would have the strength to leave her this time. He wanted her too damned much.

She took his hand again, leading him over to the mirror. He watched their reflection as she stood beside him, running her hands over him, unbuttoning his shirt, tugging the shirttails from his dress slacks. His eyes were glued to the mirror, watching the image of her undressing him as if it was someone else, a show he was watching rather than part of. Except that every tingle of response, every shudder of pleasure as her hands moved over him was real.

She slipped her hands inside his shirt and rubbed them over his chest, where she was sure to feel the slamming of his heart against his ribs. Heat moved over him in waves. Her mouth followed her hands, and before he knew it he was naked in front of the mirror, his body glistening with sweat, rock hard and fully aroused.

He stared at the image of her kneeling in front of him, and when her reflection showed her leaning forward to touch her mouth to him, he gritted his teeth to hold on to his tattered control and nearly shouted out the truth, but desire robbed him of speech, and only her name came out on a long moan.

Her lips closed over him and his thighs tensed with the sharp pleasure of it. She was improvising a bit, but he wasn't about to argue. He dropped his head back as she dragged her mouth over him, releasing him from her hot mouth into the cool air of the room. She rose, took him by the hand again and led him to the bed.

"Sit." Her breathing was shallow and he knew she was as aroused as he was. His heart fell while his passion rose even higher as he watched her kick off her shoes and peel off the lacy nightgown that had haunted his memories. She was going to let it happen—they were going to make love.

And he wanted it to happen. There was no way now

that he could refuse her. He loved her and he wanted her—needed her like he needed to breathe. But then his mind spun out the future...perhaps the lie between them would fade over time...maybe in the long run it wouldn't make a difference? Maybe sometimes the end did justify the means? The thoughts raced torrentially through his mind, but in his heart, he knew he didn't believe it.

He ached as he watched her and he knew he couldn't let this happen again, no matter how much he loved her and wanted her, he was going to stop, just as he had that first evening.

It all felt too cruel, as if they were caught in some inevitable loop that always ended with him walking out the door. The last time he had gone walking and ended up in the harbor with amnesia, but where would he go this time? What was left without her?

Standing before him in only a silky, flesh-toned thong, she met his gaze with such desire, such openness, and...*tears.* He blinked. She hadn't cried before. But now, tears streamed down her cheeks and she faced him, the palms of her hands open toward him, her eyes pleading, and he felt his heart break with it.

"Colin, before...*if*...this happens, I have to tell you something."

He held his breath. The sense of expectation was so sharp it was painful, and he started to speak, to spare her the torment. It was enough to know she wanted to tell him. But she shushed him, sticking to her rules.

"You can't speak, remember?" Her voice quavered as

she stripped away the thong, standing before him completely naked just as he was, bared body, heart and soul. Love overwhelmed him and he rose from the bed to go to her. Wrapping his arms around her before she could speak, he held her close and overrode her objections.

"I know," he said, his voice rough in her ear.

She pushed away slightly, misunderstanding him, resisting him. "No, not like this. I need to tell you, about that night. I lied—"

He spoke more insistently, pushing her hair away from where it was plastered to her tearstained cheeks. God, she was so beautiful he could hardly bear it.

"I *know,* Miranda. I know what happened that night."

She drew back, blinking in astonishment and confusion. "It worked? You mean this reenactment brought your memory back? Just like that?"

He shook his head, grimacing as he exposed his own deception. "No, it returned before—about a week ago, during our trip."

Her arms fell to her sides, and she turned a few shades paler, looking at him in disbelief. "You…you remembered? You knew? All this time?"

He held her eyes steadily. "Yes. I knew. I knew I left that night. And that we, um, didn't actually make love."

"Why didn't you say anything? Why didn't you tell me?"

She wrapped her arms around herself as she moved to sit on the edge of the bed, where she stared up at him, questioning.

"I had to think. When I realized things hadn't happened between us exactly as you said they did, I was shocked, and I didn't know what to do about it. I was angry you had lied to me." He kept his voice calm, though his breath felt short.

"So you decided to lie to me back? To get even? Is that what this is about?"

"No! No, sweetheart, nothing like that. I love you. I've never stopped loving you, not for a second, but I needed to know. I needed to find out if you would..."

"Continue living the lie..." Awareness dawned in her eyes.

Colin nodded, ashamed. "Yes, I'm so sorry, Randi... I just didn't know—"

She shushed him again, shaking her head and blinking back tears. "No, no apologies, Colin. I understand why you did what you did. I never should have lied to you in the first place, but I did want to tell you. I tried..."

He nodded, taking her ice-cold hands in his. "I know...."

"But things moved so fast, and I hadn't thought it through. I didn't know we would...that I would..."

His eyes warmed. "Fall as hard as we did?"

She nodded, her eyes bleak. "I'm so sorry I lied to you, Colin. But I can't say I'm sorry about what we've shared. I wouldn't trade a moment of it, even though it started on a lie. I do love you, that's the truth. Every moment I've had with you since that first lie has been truthful. I want you to know that."

He kissed her forehead. "You're talking as if it's

all over, in the past. Aren't you interested in a future with me?"

She blinked, not quite sure she was hearing what she thought she was. "You still want to be with me? You're not leaving?" *Again,* she thought silently.

He laughed softly then, and hugged her tight.

"Miranda, I couldn't imagine walking out on you any more than I could imagine stopping breathing. I'll admit, it threw me for a loop that you, uh, rewrote our history a little bit, and I didn't want us to always have lies between us, mine or yours." He chuckled against her hair, his warm breath sending a tingle over her skin. "But we've both been a couple of idiots, haven't we? I should've let you know how I felt so long ago. And I was a damned fool to leave you that night. It'll never happen again. Shouldn't have happened then, won't happen now. I love you and I'm not going anywhere. Ever."

Suddenly Miranda was tantalizingly aware that they were sitting so close to each other, completely nude. His words seeped into her brain then wrapped around her heart. *He still loved her. He wanted to be with her.* Relief, happiness and arousal surged through her all at once and she threw herself into his arms, knocking him backward on the bed, laughing.

"Colin, I've been so afraid all this time that I screwed things up so badly. I love you, I love you so much!" She laid half over him, planting kisses everywhere she could reach, laving his skin with her tongue, and his laugh turned to a heavy moan. He tried to separate himself, just for a moment.

"I do have something I wanted to ask you, though."

"Later." Her breath was hot on his skin, and he writhed underneath her.

"I'd rather not wait."

Just then, the phone rang, and they drew back from each other, considering for a moment, then Miranda shook her head.

"Let it ring."

He agreed and she smiled, falling forward again to pick up where she had left off when the answering machine clicked on. Try as they might to ignore it, the excited laughter and loud voices of Travis and Penny filled the room as they shouted out that they were getting married, causing Miranda and Colin to break apart, both of them diving for the phone, laughing.

Miranda got there first.

"You're *what?*" she nearly shouted into the receiver.

Colin looked on and could hear their happy voices from where he stood close by, bursting out laughing when Travis boasted that Penny had proposed to him, but that he'd made her get down on one knee and do it again before he said yes. Leave it to those two.

Miranda's eyes crinkled with laughter, but as she leisurely let her gaze travel over Colin's naked and still aroused body, she reached out to touch him. She wrapped her hand around the rigid length of him teasingly while she listened to their happy friends on the other end of the phone. Suffering the wonderful torture of her hands for a few silent moments, he finally took the phone away from her, trying to control his voice as he said goodbye.

"Congrats, guys—we'll meet you for breakfast." He grinned. "Yes, Trav, I'm hanging up now. Don't call back, okay?" Miranda heard Travis's knowing laughter across the line as she stroked Colin a little faster.

"Good for them."

Colin groaned, covering her hand with his. "Good for me."

Miranda caught her breath, seeing all the love and passion Colin had for her there for the taking. She planned to start taking—and giving—right now. Walking him backward, she pushed him gently onto the bed, meaning to finish the seduction she had originally planned.

"You know, I had plans for you that night that I never got around to. I think we should follow through on that reenactment idea and rewrite history—again. What d'ya think?"

Colin's eyes were hot on her as she ran her hands over her body, massaging her breasts, leaning over to drag her stiff nipples across his stomach, her eyes taunting him with the possibilities.

"Miranda…?"

"Yes, Colin."

He smiled, his face contorted in pleasure as she lifted up and slid down over him, sheathing him deeply within her. He struggled to form words as she pressed down tightly and then pulled back slowly, sensual glee shining in her eyes.

"You don't…*ahhhhh*…you don't know what I was going to ask…."

She felt him growing harder and more insistent inside of her, her own insides tensing and melting simultaneously as the urge for release built.

"It doesn't matter…later…just…oh!"

Flipping her over neatly, Colin slipped off the edge of the bed and stood facing her. Pulling her hips forward, he bent her knees, pressing her legs back as he drove into her deeper, harder, pushing them both toward heaven. He watched her come, fell in love with the passionate abandon, the complete openness she offered him. Then he returned the gift by letting her watch him as he let go as well.

It was stunning, and he couldn't believe it could ever get better between them, though he was anxious to find out. Breathing hard, he smiled. Their skin was slick with sweat and sex, and he pulled her back up close to him, nestling her head against his chest.

"I guess we might want to talk to Pen and Travis about a double wedding. If that's okay with you?"

"That would be perfect." Miranda threw arms and legs around him in sheer joy. "I guess everything did work out after all, didn't it?"

Colin laughed, seeking her mouth for a hot kiss. "It did. Even better than we imagined."

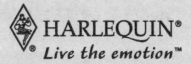

DYNASTIES: THE ASHTONS

**A family built on lies...
brought together by dark,
passionate secrets.**

JUST A TASTE

(Silhouette Desire #1645,
available April 2005)

by Bronwyn Jameson

When Jillian Ashton's arrogant
husband died, it wasn't long before
she found a man who treated her
right—*really* right. Problem was,
Seth—a tall, dark and handsome
hunk—was her late husband's
brother. She'd planned on just
a taste of his tender touch, but
was left wanting more....

*Available at your
favorite retail outlet.*

Blaze

HARLEQUIN *Blaze*™

If you loved her story
GOOD TIME GIRL,
you'll go crazy for

THE COWBOY WAY
by **Candace Schuler**
Blaze #177

Jo Beth Jensen is practical. Burned once by a
cowboy, she swore never to get involved with another
one. But sexy Clay Madison is different. A champion
rodeo bull rider, Clay is just too easy on the eyes to
ignore. Although she knows she should steer clear,
Jo Beth can't help herself. Her body needs some sexual
relief, and the cowboy way is the only way to go....

Available April 2005.
On sale at your favorite retail outlet.

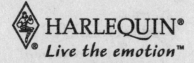

HARLEQUIN®
Live the emotion™

Blaze

HARLEQUIN® Blaze™

Get ready to check in to Hush...

Piper Devon has opened a hot new hotel that caters to the senses...and it's giving ex-lover Trace Winslow a few sleepless nights.

Check out

#178 HUSH

by Jo Leigh

Available April 2005

Book #1, Do Not Disturb miniseries

Look for linked stories by Isabel Sharpe, Alison Kent, Nancy Warren, Debbi Rawlins and Jill Shalvis in the months to come!

Shhh...Do Not Disturb

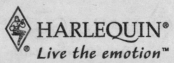

HARLEQUIN®
Live the emotion™